MUDDLE EARTH TOO
THE TROUBLE WITH BIG SISTERS

D0807581

MUDDLE EARTH TOO

THE TROUBLE WITH BIG SISTERS

Paul Stewart &
Chris Riddell

First published in Great Britain in 2011
by Macmillan Children's Books
This Large Print edition published 2012
by AudioGO Ltd
by arrangement with
Macmillan Publishers Limited

ISBN: 978 1445 842240

British Library Cataloguing in Publication Data available

Printed and bound in Great Britain by
MPG Books Group Limited

For Julie
PS

For Jo
CR

NAME: Joe Jefferson

OCCUPATION: Schoolboy

HOBBIES: Football, TV, arguing with his sister

FAVOURITE FOOD: Anything not cooked by Norbert

NAME: Randalf the Wise, Muddle Earth's . . . er, leading wizard?

OCCUPATION: Wizard Headmaster of Stinkyhogs School of Wizardry

HOBBIES: Performing spells (I think you'll find that's spell! – Veronica)

FAVOURITE FOOD: Norbert's squashed tadpole fritters

NAME: Ella Jefferson

OCCUPATION: Moody big sister to her brother, Joe – and a barbarian princess

HOBBIES: See 'Occupation', plus painting her nails black

FAVOURITE FOOD: Cheeseburger and fries

NAME: Norbert the
Not-Very-Big
OCCUPATION: School cook
HOBBIES: Thumb-sucking,
cooking – especially
cake-decorating
FAVOURITE FOOD:
Everything

NAME: Veronica
OCCUPATION: Familiar to the
great wizard, Randalf the Wise
HOBBIES: Being sarcastic
FAVOURITE FOOD:
Anything not cooked by Norbert

NAME: Walter, once The
Horned Baron, now retired
OCCUPATION: Retired Ruler
of Muddle Earth
HOBBIES: Wooing Fifi the Fair
in their love nest in Trollbridge
FAVOURITE FOOD: Bad-
breath porridge

NAME: Lord Asbow
OCCUPATION: Dean of
University of Whatever
HOBBIES: Repelling invaders,
discussing the meaning of life
with his pet Labrador
FAVOURITE FOOD: Sunrise dust,
dog food

NAME: Edward Gorgeous

OCCUPATION: Student and barbarian

HOBBIES: Broomball, brooding, looking gorgeous

FAVOURITE FOOD: Tomatoes (sort of)

NAME: Edwina Lovely

OCCUPATION: Queen Susan's lady-in-waiting (sometimes)

HOBBIES: Looking lovely, obsessing over Edward Gorgeous

FAVOURITE FOOD: Royal blood

NAME: Eraguff the Eager-to-Please

OCCUPATION: Dragon

HOBBIES: Nest decorating, flower picking, knitting

FAVOURITE FOOD: Definitely NOT wizard

NAME: Eudora Pinkwhistle, one of Muddle Earth's leading witches

OCCUPATION: Potions teacher, Stinkyhogs

HOBBIES: Spells, and crushing on a certain wizard headmaster

FAVOURITE FOOD: Tea and fairy-cake

NAME: Mr Fluffy

OCCUPATION: Woodwork teacher, Stinkyhogs

HOBBIES: Storing food in his chubby cheeks, howling at Muddle Earth's three moons

FAVOURITE FOOD: Nuts

NAME: Kings Peter and Edmund and Queens Susan and Lucy

OCCUPATION: Er . . . Kings and Queens

HOBBIES:
Bossing people about

FAVOURITE FOOD: As long as it's expensive, anything!

NAME: Pesticide and Nettle, Thistle and Briar Rose

OCCUPATION: Flower fairies

HOBBIES: Jeer-leading, causing trouble

FAVOURITE FOOD:
Pollen pizza

BOOK TWO

The Trouble with Big Sisters!

PROLOGUE

'Once upon a very long time ago, there lived a messy and muddled ruler, Marthur of the Round Kitchen Table. Bold of biscuit and light of sponge, his fondants were fancy and his buns were iced. Throughout the land of Muddle, his prowess with a waffle iron and his skill with a cake-slice were legendary and celebrated in song.

'Though his pots are burned and his
pans are gritty,
His cakes are fair and his pastries
pretty;
His kitchen's a shambles and his
stove's a mess,
But good King Marthur couldn't
care less.

'But woe is me, gentle reader, for it came to pass that the kitchen did fill up with a heap of cutlery and crockery and cooking utensils of every description. Verily was the floor strewn with baking trays and pots and pans, both short and long of handle, until there was, forsooth, a veritable mountain of washing-up.

'"Alas and alack!" cried King Marthur, attempting to find a clean plate. "I give up."

'He seized his sword and plunged it into a freshly baked scone of prodigious size and unparalleled deliciousness that he had just that moment pulled from the oven. As he strode from the kitchen, never to return, he spoke these immortal words:

'"Let he who pulls the sword from the scone do the washing-up and become the new and rightful ruler of the Round Kitchen Table . . . I'm off!"

'Many and varied were the bakers, the pastry-cooks and cake-decoraters who took up this legendary challenge, but all to no avail. Try as they might, none could pull the mighty sword from the floury dough-based teatime favourite. And they all lived happily ever after.

'Alas and alack! Alack and alas, dear reader. For this is a sad and sorry tale indeed, and had I hands to wring, I would surely wring them well and truly in the telling of it. But I have no hands. All I have are these beautifully written and magnificently illustrated pages that you see before you, and of course my mellifluous storytelling voice, with which to beguile and enchant you . . .

'Did I hear you right, gentle reader? You wish to hear my tale again? Very well! Once upon a very long time—'

'No, I don't!' said Joe, grabbing the book that was fluttering in the air above him like a moth over a candle, and slamming it shut. 'Fourteen times is quite enough. Will you please stay on your shelf and leave me alone. I'm trying to think!'

He climbed to his feet, crossed the room and placed the book firmly back on the shelf.

'Be like that then,' muttered the

book huffily.

Joe turned away and was about to return to the wing-backed chair where he'd been sitting for the last half-hour, trying to collect his thoughts. Where was the Goblet of Porridge—and the lamp-post, for that matter? And where was *Ella*? Could she really be in league with Edward and the jeer-leaders in their dastardly scheme to steal the goblet? And as for the lamp-post, even if he did locate it, and the portal, how could he go back without Ella?

That was the trouble with big sisters. They were so unreliable: swooning over handsome strangers and disappearing with them on battlecats . . .

'*There* you are,' said Roger the Wrinkled, who had just walked into the library and spotted the book.

Not that that was difficult, since there were only three other books on the dusty bookshelves: *Mucky Maud's Songbook*, *The Horned Helmet Autumn Catalogue* and *Binky the Bunny's Big Birthday Surprise*.

'I've been looking for you everywhere,' said Roger as he picked

6

the book up and placed it in the pocket of his flowery chemise. 'Oh, and what have we here?' he added, picking up *Binky the Bunny's Big Birthday Surprise*. 'I do enjoy a good thriller.'

7

Looking up, the wizard saw Joe and frowned. 'Still here?' he said. 'Shouldn't you and Randalf have set off on the quest to find the Goblet of Porridge by now? After all, there's no time to lose, you know. Not if you want the school to stay open . . .'

'Do *you* wish to hear my tale, gentle reader?' the book piped up.

'Oh, yes,' said Roger the Wrinkled enthusiastically, settling himself down in a chair. 'Let me get comfortable, then you can begin.'

The wind was up, whipping the sand and dust into the air and fuzzing the yellow and purple moons. The mighty battlecat flinched and yowled with unease, the fur at its neck and shoulders standing on end.

'Easy, Tiddles,' whispered the handsome youth upon its back, leaning forward and smoothing its ruffled fur.

The girl seated behind him shivered

and tightened her black-fingernailed hold around his waist.

'Where are we?' she asked as lightning suddenly crackled and flashed above her head.

The youth turned. Another flash of lightning illuminated his high cheekbones, his sculpted jaw, and glinted in his red-tinged, almond-shaped eyes. He took the girl's hands in his and squeezed gently. He held her trembling gaze.

The howling wind and crashing thunder sounded like the clashing chords played upon a mighty organ.

'Nowhere,' he whispered.

'There you are!' said Roger the Wrinkled, frowning with irritation at Randalf, who was sitting at the top of the main staircase of Stinkyhogs, his faithful ogre servant, Norbert, seated on the stair below.

They were both dressed for travel, wearing cloaks and carrying luggage. Randalf had the stoutest staff from the staff room in his hand and a small backpack on his shoulders, while Norbert was holding a small leather satchel. Veronica the budgie was ready too, with a tiny scarf knotted at her neck, a miniature bobble hat on her head and a pair of little boots on her feet. She was perched in her favourite spot on the brim of Randalf's pointy hat.

'I've brought my recipe book *and* my

10

findy bag,' said Norbert, his triple eyes blinking in sequence as he smiled down at Roger the Wrinkled and Joe at the foot of the staircase.

He unbuckled the small leather satchel and rootled about inside it. 'This is where I keep my souvenirs,' he explained. 'Like this fabulous jewel of solid pebble,' he said, raising a small dull grey pebble between his finger and thumb. 'And this exquisite can of finest tin.' He held up a rusty tin can. 'And this—'

'I get the idea,' said Roger the Wrinkled, tapping the toe of his red high-heeled shoe impatiently. He looked up at Randalf. 'I can't tell you the fuss the kings and queens are making over this Goblet of Porridge business. It makes us wizards look so bad . . . I'm counting on you, Randalf, as headmaster of Stinkyhogs School of Wizardry, to put everything right. You've got the school holidays to find the goblet and bring it back to the school trophy-cabinet so we can put a stop to King Peter's petulant sighs and Queen Susan's sulky silences, not to mention Queen Lucy's filthy looks and King Edmund's flatulence . . .'

'Leave it to me, Roger, sir,' said Randalf confidently. He paused. 'There's just one thing . . .'

'Well?' said Roger wearily.

'It's this,' said Randalf. He tapped the brown stair-carpet on which he and Norbert were sitting. 'I think it's broken.'

'What do you mean, broken?'

'It won't fly,' said Randalf.

'It's a *magic* carpet,' said Roger. 'One that requires *magic* to make it fly.' He sighed. 'I can't think why *you* can't make it work.'

'No, sir, neither can I . . .'

'That was sarcasm.' Roger sighed again. 'I've worn petticoats with more talent for magic than you possess, Randalf.'

Randalf went red in the face. 'I . . . I employed an aeronautical betwitching spell of the highest calibre,' he blustered.

'I'm not sure that hitting it with your staff and shouting "Fly, you blasted thing!" counts,' said Veronica.

'Quite,' said Roger, rolling his eyes. 'What is required, Randalf—as you would know, if you had paid any attention when you were my apprentice—is a spell of transportation, a subtle and sensitive spell . . .' He stared down at the stair-carpet.

It was long and thin and frayed at the edges. Once it had been patterned. Now, grubby, worn and badly faded, it was brown. Plain brown. Apart from the stains.

'Let your weave be wafted and your weft upraised,' Roger intoned, sweeping back his sleeve and pointing at the rug. 'And your zephyr-light wool to the skies be praised!'

The carpet gave a soft put-upon sigh and seemed to shrug. Then, as Joe watched, it raised itself slowly into the air, a step at a time, until it hovered, kinked at right angles, above the staircase.

'Now what?' said Randalf from the top step of the floating stair-carpet.

'Flatter, signal, manoeuvre,' said Roger patiently.

13

'Do what?' said Randalf.

'Standard flying procedure,' said Roger, helping Joe up on to the carpet. 'Say something nice to it,' he instructed. 'Tap the bottom step lightly with your staff and give the command, "Fly!"'

Randalf nodded uncertainly.

'Ready?' Roger the Wrinkled asked.

'Leaving without me, you naughty, naughty wizard?' came a lovely voice.

Everyone turned to see Edwina Lovely walking down the school corridor in an ankle-length cloak with a fur-trimmed hood and matching handbag, her lovely eyes wide and her lovelier black hair tied back in a fetching ponytail. She stopped in front of the hovering stair-carpet and put her lovely hands on her lovely hips.

'I promised Queen Susan that I would help you in your quest, wizard,' she told Randalf, 'and help you I shall.'

She jumped on to the bottom step of the carpet and sat down next to Joe.

'Isn't this exciting?' she said, and gave a delightful tinkling laugh.

'If you're *quite* ready, Randalf,' said Roger the Wrinkled, an irritated edge to his voice.

'Ready and raring to go, sir,' Randalf confirmed unconvincingly. He cleared his throat, whacked the stair-carpet with his staff and roared, *'Fly!'*

The carpet reared up.

'Whooooah!'

A loud cry echoed round the hall as everyone was thrown violently back and had to hold on tightly to the frayed edges of the carpet as it flew down the corridor.

'Waaaaah!'

An even louder cry went up. The heavy oak doors they were heading for were closed. Roger the Wrinkled calmly raised a hand, clicked his fingers, and the doors burst open.

'Wheeeee!' squealed Norbert as the

flying stair-carpet swept through the doorway and outside.

'Hold on to your hats!' Randalf shouted, doing just that with one hand while, with the other, he gripped the front of the stair-carpet.

The flying carpet shot up high into the sky, then swooped back down and began speeding round the walls of the Horned Baron's castle. In the castle doorway, Roger the Wrinkled's wrinkled face and flapping hands flashed past in a blur, once, twice, three times . . .

'We're going round in circles!' Randalf groaned. 'What's the matter with the stupid thing?'

Instantly, the flying carpet jerked back and sighed a sort of if-you're-going-to-be-like-that kind of sigh, before rippling limply as it slowed to a halt and floated to the ground like a ribbon on the wind. It landed with a bump and a cloud of dust on the castle doorstep, where Roger the Wrinkled stood, clicking his red high-heels together in irritation.

'Flatter, signal, manoeuvre,' he said.

'You forgot to say something nice—and you were *far* too heavy with your staff. And as for your command . . .'

'*And* he called the carpet stupid,' said Veronica, smoothing down her feathers and adjusting her bobble hat.

'Now, perhaps you'd like to try that again, Randalf,' said Roger testily.

Randalf looked down at the carpet. 'Errm, "stupid"? Did I say "stupid"?' he said. 'A slip of the tongue. I meant . . . *stupendous*. I meant *superb*. I meant that you are a *superlative* carpet, beautifully woven, intelligent, graceful, and not at all stained . . .'

'All right, don't overdo it,' Veronica interrupted.

Not one to bear a grudge, the flying stair-carpet rose up in the air once more and its passengers gripped on tightly to their respective steps. Holding his staff gingerly by his fingertips, Randalf lightly tapped the stair-carpet and purred in a soft, sing-song voice, 'Fly!'

With a gentle that's-more-like-it kind of sigh, the stair-carpet flew back up into the sky and circled round the

17

pointy towers of the castle.

'Now tell it where you want to go,' Roger called up to Randalf.

'Ogres love a good gossip,' said Edwina Lovely, snuggling up close to Joe on the bottom step. 'We're bound to find out something in the Ogre Hills.'

'That's just what I was thinking,' said Randalf, puffing out his chest importantly. 'Please take us to the Ogre Hills, fair rug of unparalleled loveliness.'

Instantly, the stair-carpet stopped circling the towers of the castle and set off across the sky towards the far horizon.

'And do feel free to take your time,' Randalf added, pulling his pointy hat down low over his eyes and folding his arms, 'O stair covering of legendary magnificence.' He yawned.

Once again, the stair-carpet did as it was requested. It slowed down to a soft, rippling speed and its passengers let out sighs of their own and began to relax.

'As I was saying to Queen Susan,

it all seems perfectly clear to me,'
said Edwina Lovely, slipping the
red ribbon from her lovely hair and
letting the dark tresses cascade over
her shoulders. 'Edward Gorgeous
planned the whole thing. It was his
idea to challenge Golden Towers
to the broomball match, just so we
would bring the Goblet of Porridge
to Stinkyhogs. And he recruited those
jeer-leaders to steal the goblet while he
kept us all distracted. Then he made
his getaway on a stolen battlecat with
that black-fingernailed lummox!'

'That wasn't a lummox,' said Norbert indignantly. 'That was Joe's big sister, Ella. She and Edward are an item—at least, that's what I heard Eloise Wolfbane say, who heard it from Sophie Skullsplitter, who said Lynda the Barbarianette told her . . .'

'You see,' said Edwina, with a petulant toss of her head. She turned away and Joe got a faceful of lovely hair. 'Ogres have all the best gossip. Even the stupidest ones like Numbutt here. In the Ogre Hills we're bound to find out something about Edward's whereabouts . . .'

'His name's Norbert,' spluttered Joe, pushing Edwina's hair aside and moving to the next step up, 'and he's right. Ella isn't a *lummox*—whatever that might be. She's just an ordinary girl. She isn't interested in the Goblet of Porridge . . . All I know is that I've got to find her, so that the pair of us can return home.'

But Edwina Lovely was no longer listening. Instead, her lovely hands were gripping the sides of the stair-carpet and her lovely face had a far from lovely sneer on it.

'Edward, Edward, Edward,' she muttered, gazing into the middle distance. 'Do you really think you can hide from me? Don't you know I will always find you in the end, wherever you run, whatever you do . . . whoever you're with! And when I do . . .' She trembled, her eyes sparkling and her face a deathly white. For a moment she sat still as a statue, before suddenly seeming to remember where she was. She looked over her shoulder at Joe and Norbert and gave that tinkling little laugh of hers. 'Sorry,' she said, 'I don't know what came over me.'

'You want to watch her,' Veronica whispered as she jumped on to Joe's shoulder. 'Not quite right in the head if you ask me.'

From the top stair, there came the sound of snoring. Randalf was fast asleep.

The flying carpet flew on, leaving the Musty Mountains far behind them, Mount Boom gently *boom-boom-booming* in the distance. Joe looked up. The Enchanted Lake was rapidly approaching and he could make out the seven houseboats belonging to the wizards of Muddle Earth bobbing on its sparkling surface. Floating in mid-air, the lake was an extraordinary sight, with the Enchanted River flowing down from it and looking like the stalk of a mighty mushroom.

'Only in Muddle Earth,' muttered Joe to himself, shaking his head.

A waft of pungent perfume filled the air with the scent of a thousand trampled rose petals mixed with the aroma of a million bruised violets, and the faintest whiff of pink stinky hog. Joe looked down. They were now passing over the Perfumed Bog. Far below, in the pink perfumed mist a pink stinky hog raised its curly tail and broke wind. Joe held his nose.

A while later, the bog gave way to flat, dusty ground, scattered with grassy mounds that gradually grew in size and number. Soon they were flying across an undulating landscape of barren hills.

'Wake up, sir. We're here,' said Norbert excitedly, shaking Randalf by the shoulders. 'The Ogre Hills!' His three eyes glistened as he looked at an endless expanse of dry, dusty hillocks. 'Isn't it beautiful!'

'Those aren't my pantaloons, and the cabbages are in the bath . . .' Randalf muttered sleepily. His eyes snapped open. 'Where am I?'

'The Ogre Hills, Fatso,' said Veronica, hopping from Joe's shoulder and on to Randalf's hat. 'Pull yourself together. We need you to land this thing . . . Politely!'

The wizard yawned and stretched extravagantly. 'O floor-tapestry of undreamt delight, if you'd be so good as to descend, I should be eternally grateful.'

With a little sigh, the stair-carpet swooped down out of the sky and came to a halt inches from the ground, maintaining its stair-like shape.

'Thank you, wondrous woven one,' said Randalf, climbing to his feet and stepping down the stairs. 'Follow me, everyone.'

But Edwina Lovely had beaten him to it, and was already striding purposefully towards a group of gigantic figures in the distance. As she approached, the five ogres turned and glowered down at her, their triple eyes narrowing suspiciously.

'What's the word in the hills?' she said brightly, tossing back her mane of lovely hair.

'Who wants to know?' growled a massive ogre in a grubby custard-stained vest, a blue velveteen rabbit tucked under one hairy armpit.

'Oh, my, what an adorable bunny-wunny,' Edwina Lovely simpered. 'You must be so proud.'

'You mean Gilbert?' said the ogre, giving a shy, green-tusked smile. He raised the velveteen rabbit to his stubbled cheek and rubbed it up and down. 'He *is* very soft and snuggly.'

'And tell me, Gilbert,' said Edwina, perching daintily on a boulder and staring intently at the velveteen rabbit, 'with those lovely big ears of yours, have you heard any talk of a tall handsome stranger hiding in these parts?'

The ogre put the velveteen rabbit to his ear and listened intently. 'Gilbert

24

says *he* hasn't heard anything,' he said, shaking his head solemnly. 'But he thinks that Elly-Welly might have.'

The even more enormous ogre next to him held the patchwork elephant he was cradling to his ear. 'Elly-Welly ain't seen nuffink.'

'Maisie hasn't either,' announced a slightly smaller ogre with a misshapen knitted mouse in his hand.

'Nor has Sebastian,' said an ogre with a teddy bear.

'And Blanky keeps himself to himself,' said the smallest ogre of the bunch, who was clutching a small chewed-looking blanket.

'So much for gossiping ogres,' Veronica retorted from the brim of Randalf's hat, as the wizard came striding up to Edwina Lovely and stopped beside her, breathing hard.

Behind him, Norbert the Not-Very-Big ogre, suddenly all shy and bashful, squeezed Joe's hand and looked down at the ground.

'Oh, my goodness, what a magnificent snuggly-wuggly,' said the smallest ogre, who was still nearly twice as big as Norbert, as he stared at the rolled-up stair-carpet that Randalf was holding under his arm. 'Can I hold it? Can I stroke it? Oh, it looks so soft and cuddly . . .'

'No, *I* want to . . .'

'No, me . . . me . . .'

26

The ogres crowded in around them, their triple eyes wide and yellow-tinged tusks gleaming menacingly.

'Headmaster? Headmaster, is that you?'

'Bradley the Big-For-His-Age?' said Randalf as the Stinkyhogs School broomball player came bounding up to them. The young ogre stopped and frowned. 'Dorian the Dribbler! Leave the headmaster alone! And you, Nicholas the Nappy Filler, you wait till I tell your mummy! And the rest of you, you ought to be ashamed!'

The enormous ogres hung their heads and stroked their snuggly-wugglies furiously.

'Sorry . . . Sorry . . . Sorry . . .' came a chorus of deep ogre voices.

'So what brings you to the Ogre Hills?' Bradley asked brightly, turning to Randalf and the others.

'We're searching for Edward Gorgeous,' said Edwina Lovely, stepping boldly towards him. 'He's a team-mate of yours,' she said accusingly. 'You're not hiding him, are you?'

'Of course not,' said Bradley, taken aback. 'I haven't seen Edward since just after Tinklebell shouted the final whistle and the crowd invaded the pitch.' He shrugged. 'After the game, I came home for the holidays. The last thing I remember is looking over the heads of the crowd and seeing him whisper something in Smutley's ear. The next moment, he was gone.' He blinked tearfully, once, twice, and then again. 'You don't really think that Edward stole the goblet, do you?'

'The Edward Gorgeous *I* know is capable of anything,' said Edwina darkly.

'Just how well *do* you know Edward Gorgeous?' asked Joe.

But Edwina Lovely ignored him. 'Come, wizard!' she announced bossily. 'Roll out that carpet of yours. We're off to find Smutley in Goblintown!'

A narrow, dusty road wound its way through a parched and empty landscape, heading north from the Musty Mountains. Far to the east, like a crazily over-decorated birthday cake topped with a thousand twisted candles, was the walled city of Goblintown with its tall towers and smoking chimneys. To the west, dark mountains rose on the distant horizon.

A lone serpent, high in the sky, flapped its ragged wings as it made its way over the jagged peaks. A little way to the left, another lone serpent flew slowly past. And a little way left of that, a third lone serpent lumbered laboriously across the sky. And a little way to the left of *that* was another and another and another—for here, and here, and here, be dragons.

29

The road continued northwards to the very edge of the map, where it petered out next to a small signpost, which bore the neatly painted words, *WELCOME TO NOWHERE— Twinned with WHATEVER*. Beyond, the uncharted barbarian lands of the north stretched as far as the eye could see.

'Left a bit. Left a bit. Right a bit. Throw! . . . By the twin orbs of Wotulf the Stormbringer, that was a fine effort for one so untutored.'

'Ooh, do you think so? Can I have another go?'

The barbarian princess reached out a black-fingernailed hand and picked up a second battleaxe. Bracing her legs at the knees, she raised the axe high above her head and took aim at the lemon drizzle cake propped up against the rock a little way off. Swinging her arm athletically, she let go of the axe, sending it spinning towards the target. With a heavy thud, the double-edged battleaxe embedded itself in the centre of the cake, scattering crumbs in all directions.

'Good shot, fair maiden!' exclaimed the hulking barbarian standing by her side. He scratched his thick ginger beard thoughtfully. 'Let's see, you've mastered battle-roaring, swordplay and axe-throwing, now what about a spot of battlecat taming?'

'Battlecats!' said Ella. 'I'd like that! But only if you think I'm ready, Deric.'

Deric the Red threw back his head and gave a roar of barbarian laughter, loud and hearty behind white clenched teeth.

'Ready? Why, by the whiskers of Freya the Beardy, you're a natural, young Ella. Follow me.'

They turned from the axe-range and made their way along a track that led them through a wooded valley. Tall pine trees studded the rocky slopes to their right and left, a waterfall of crystal-clear mountain water cascaded down into a limpid pool before them, and beyond that lay alpine meadows dotted with yak-skin tents of various shapes and sizes. At the centre of the valley stood a magnificent wooden hall, with ornately carved lintels, onion-

31

domed towers and a mighty pillared archway that framed two huge, black-hinged doors.

Ella followed Deric the Red round the edge of the pool and out across the meadow beyond, towards the tents. Deric paused beside a large patchwork yurt of stitched-together hides, some shaggy and new, some smooth and worn, but all smelling of damp yak.

'Excuse me for a moment,' he said, pulling aside a hairy tent-flap and disappearing inside. There came the sound of pots clattering and wooden chests being rummaged through. A minute later, Deric emerged with a jug and saucer in one hand and a large ball of yak wool in the other. 'This way,' he said cheerfully, his winged helmet wobbling on his head as he nodded towards the nearby meadow.

Ella followed him, catching her reflection in a burnished barbarian shield propped up against a neighbouring tent as she did so. She paused for a moment. She had to admit, she certainly looked the part, with her white-feathered helmet, blonde plaits, tooled-leather breastplate, short pleated barbarian skirt and barbarian sandals cross-laced to the knee.

'Here, kitty, kitty, kitty,' came Deric's bellowing voice.

Ella tore herself away from her reflection and hurried across to the barbarian. Deric the Red was pouring yak's milk from the jug into the saucer he'd placed on the ground at his feet. He stepped back.

'Here, kitty, kitty,' he bellowed.

Out from the dappled shadows of the wooded slopes came an excited roar and the sound of pounding feet as a huge pink-striped creature burst into the meadow. With its broad shoulders, rippling muscles and great sabre-toothed snarl, the cat was twice the size of Tiddles, the battlecat that Edward had 'borrowed' from the stables at Stinkyhogs.

'Careful now,' said Deric gravely. 'They can sense it if you're afraid.'

'I'm not afraid,' said Ella, smiling.

The huge cat came to a halt before them, a growl rumbling at the back

of its throat. It fixed Ella with a fiery
stare, before lowering its head and
sniffing tentatively at the saucer. It shot
out a long pink tongue, tasted the milk
and began lapping. The growl turned
to a purr.

Ella reached out and tickled the
cat between the ears. The purr grew
louder.

'You've got a way with battlecats,'

34

said Deric approvingly. 'Here, try this.' He handed her the ball of yak wool.

The fearsome beast looked up, milk dripping from its luxuriant whiskers. Behind it, its mighty tail swished to and fro. It raised a powerful paw and batted at the ball of wool, knocking it from Ella's hands and sending it rolling out across the meadow. With a roaring *miaow*, the pink-striped cat pounced on the unravelling wool, seized it in its claws and rolled on to its back. Ella laughed delightedly and rushed over to tickle its tummy.

'You're just a great big pussycat, aren't you?' she said, as the mighty battlecat's purr grew louder than ever.

'Now you've made friends,' said Deric the Red, 'why not go for a ride?'

'Really?' said Ella. 'Will it let me?'

'You're a barbarian princess with a way with battlecats,' said Deric. 'Why wouldn't it?'

Ella untangled the wool from the battlecat's claws, tickling its tummy as she did so. Climbing to its feet, the battlecat stared at her, its tail twitching expectantly.

'Go on,' said Deric. 'Jump on.'

Stroking the back of its ears, Ella pulled herself up on to the mighty creature's back. She put her arms around its neck and nuzzled its soft fur.

'Go, kitty, kitty. Go,' she whispered.

The battlecat's muscles rippled as it leaped up and galloped across the sunlit meadow. Gripping on tightly with her legs, Ella leaned forward and tickled the battlecat behind its right ear. In response, the creature turned to the right. She tickled the left ear and the creature turned left. They zigzagged round the meadow and then cantered back, coming to a stop in front of Deric as Ella pulled lightly on both the battlecat's ears at once.

'Quite astonishing.' Deric beamed, his white teeth flashing. 'Pinky's one of our biggest and fiercest battlecats. And you handled him like an expert. Well done, Ella!'

Ella slipped from the battlecat's back and stroked his soft pink fur. 'Like I said,' she giggled, 'he's just a great big pussycat. Aren't you, Pinky?'

The battlecat purred.

Just then, there came the sound of loud barbarian laughter and the drumming of galloping feet. A dozen battlecats emerged from the forest and slowed to a trot as they crossed the meadow and approached the tents. Pulling on their reins, their barbarian riders brought the battlecats to a halt and jumped from their saddles with hearty guffaws.

'By the Puddles of Asgard, my pancake batter shall not curdle this time!' said Rulf Son-of-Rulf, tying the reins of his battlecat to a tent-pole.

'Just don't ask to borrow my egg-whisk,' chuckled Glenda Daughter-of-Glenda and slapped him enthusiastically on the back.

'I've got big plans for a chocolate-chip meringue,' said Nigel Nephew-of-Nigel.

The voices of the other barbarians rose in good-natured banter as they patted their battlecats and unpacked their saddle-bags.

'Anyone seen my rolling-pin?'

'I've got a big spoon, if that'll help.'

'Last one to the Great Hall is a soggy crumpet!'

'Wait for me,' came a plaintive voice.

There was the sound of heavy *thud-thud-thud*ding and a giant lop-eared battlerabbit came hopping out of the trees and into the meadow. It paused and nibbled the grass despite the protestations of its rider, a rather weedy-looking barbarian with a wispy moustache. Wayne the Bunnyrider tugged hard on the reins.

'Come *on*, Benjamin,' he cried in frustration, 'or all the best oven gloves will be taken.'

The great black and white rabbit ignored him and continued to graze on the sweet meadow grass. With a petulant sigh, the barbarian jumped from the saddle and chased after the others.

Ella turned to Deric the Red. 'I didn't realize being a barbarian could be this much fun,' she said. 'Sword-fighting, axe-throwing and battlecat-riding out here in the middle of Nowhere . . .'

'Where no one can find us,' came a

brooding voice.

Ella spun round. 'Edward!' she exclaimed. 'Where have you been?'

'Nowhere,' he said gloomily, staring up at the wooded mountains that surrounded the valley.

'Oh, Edward, cheer up. It's so beautiful here . . .'

'Beautiful,' said Edward, taking Ella in his muscular arms and staring deep into her eyes, 'but not as beautiful as you.'

'*Ahem*,' said Deric the Red, blushing.

'I've just remembered, I've got a cake in the oven that needs seeing to. If you two will excuse me . . .'

The ginger-bearded barbarian hurried off in the direction of his tent. With a low growl, Pinky the battlecat turned on his heel and loped back across the meadow and into the forest. Neither Ella nor Edward noticed them go.

'You're still so troubled,' said Ella. 'I can see it in your eyes.'

'I've been selfish,' said Edward, shaking his head. 'I should never have allowed you to come away with me.'

'You couldn't have stopped me,' Ella said passionately. 'There's a connection between us. I felt it the very first moment you looked into my eyes. And you felt it too, don't tell me you didn't.'

'Y . . . Yes, I did. But Ella, can't you see?' Edward protested. This thing between us, it can never work. I'm not normal . . .'

'Edward, you know I don't care about *that* . . .'

'How can you not care? I am a creature of the night. A vampire. Every time I take your hand, Ella, it's as much as I can do not to suck your thumb . . .'

'No, Edward,' she protested. 'You're not a creature of the night. It's a beautiful sunny afternoon, and you're here with me.'

'But tonight, Ella . . .' he said, his gorgeous face turning a deathly white, 'while you sleep, I shall be roaming these forests looking for thumbs to suck.'

'You only suck the thumbs of stiltmice and squirrels and little rabbits,' said Ella. 'And then only when you absolutely have to.'

'It's not just that,' said Edward bleakly. 'It's my past. It's come back to haunt me. And by being with me, you're putting yourself in great danger.'

Ella tightened her grip on his arms. 'Edward,' she said, 'who *was* that girl back at the broomball pitch, the pretty one with the lovely black hair?'

Edward flinched and looked away.

'Edward,' said Ella in exasperation, 'who is she? And what *is* this danger? Tell me! Tell me. How can I help you if you won't tell me?'

41

Edward looked back at her, his pale eyes blazing red. 'Her name, if you must know,' he said, his voice trembling with emotion, 'is Edwina Lovely.' He took a deep breath. 'We first met a very long time ago . . .'

Bong! Bong! Bong! Clunk . . .

The clock at the top of the clock-tower struck four o'clock.

Bing! Bing! Bing! The clock below it struck three.

Dongle! Dongle! Dongle! Dongle! Dongle! Dongle! Dongle! Dongle! Dongle! Dongle! Dongle! Dongle! Ping! The one below that struck thirteen.

Like a wobbly stack of children's building-blocks, the clock-tower of Goblintown was made up of clocks of every description. Some were large, some were small; some resembled oversized grandfather clocks, with swinging pendulums and Roman numerals; others looked like short, stout carriage clocks, with spinning cogs and battered brass cases. Some were round, and set in wood; some

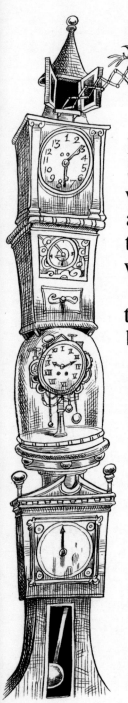

were square and set in stone. Some had thin, pointy hands and dials with no numbers, others had thick, stubby hands and numbers 1 to 13. Some had bells, some had whistles, some had klaxons and others hooters. And all of them were tolling, chiming and whistling a different hour.

At the very top of the clock-tower, two small wooden doors burst open and an elf shot out at the end of a wooden spring. He put a megaphone to his mouth.

'*Cuckoo-cuckoo!*' he called in a small, slightly petulant voice. 'And all's well . . . as can be expected.'

A goblin in the square below paused, lowered the cart he was pushing and gazed up at the clock-tower.

'Is that the time?' he said.

'Don't ask me!' The elf pinged backwards and

44

slammed the little wooden doors behind him.

'I was only asking,' the goblin muttered, picking up the wooden poles of his cart and setting off across the square to make the delivery he was probably already late for.

That was the thing about Goblintown, for the city that never slept was also the city that never kept the right time. Everyone was always late for everything. Or early. And even if they were perfectly on time, no one could ever tell.

The result was that the goblins of Goblintown ate whenever they were hungry, because they never knew when dinnertime was; slept whenever they felt like it, because they could never agree on bedtime, and smelt absolutely appalling—because bathtime was a dirty word. Whatever time of day it was, Goblintown's winding streets and narrow alleyways were filled with unwashed goblins eating snotbread sandwiches and sleeping on benches.

And as if telling the time wasn't difficult enough in Goblintown, finding space was even worse. There quite simply wasn't enough room inside the city walls, but no self-respecting goblin would dream of building his house or shop outside them. This meant that, like the clock-tower, the buildings of Goblintown were stacked one on top of the other to form tall, swaying towers, with winding stairs and crooked ladders linking one storey to the next. What's more, the towers were so tall that the cobbled streets and alleys below were cast in constant darkness and had to be lit by smelly oil-lamps.

The whole of Goblintown was full to bursting, and the pongy air rang out with a constant din of 'Ouch!' and 'Oof!' and 'Get your elbow out of my ear!' It was so cramped, there wasn't even room to swing a cat—which was a shame, since it had put paid to one of the goblins' favourite pastimes . . .

Far up at the top of the tallest tower of all, two goblin builders were busy constructing the walls of yet another precarious dwelling. They were nailing floorboards to the roof, humming tunelessly, when one of the goblins looked up.

'What do you reckon that is?' he said, pushing his filthy flat-cap back on his head and scratching his scalp.

'What do I reckon *what* is?' said his workmate.

'That.' He pointed.

Both goblins laid down their tools, climbed to their feet and looked up at the sky. They squinted into the low sun of the late afternoon, where something small and ripply seemed to be flying straight towards them.

'Is it a bird? Is it a plane? ...'

'Looks like a flying stair-carpet to me.'

'Flying a magic carpet isn't all plain sailing,' said Randalf sleepily from beneath his pointy hat.

A flock of lazybirds had just flown past, and several had landed on the carpet, yawning loudly. The wizard brushed one of them off his step with a sweep of his staff and shifted into a more comfortable position.

'How would you know when you're fast asleep most of the time?' said Veronica tartly. 'Oi! Buzz off and find your own perch!' she squawked as another lazybird flew in and attempted to settle on the brim of Randalf's hat.

The wizard began to snore.

Sitting next to Norbert on the step below, Joe looked out across the landscape of Muddle Earth. The Perfumed Bog glistened pinkly far behind them, while in the distance, the mighty Enchanted River flowed through lushly wooded countryside on its way to Trollbridge. Joe could make out the curve of the great bridge and the outline of the buildings clustered along it. Beyond Trollbridge, the hazy hump of a high hill was just visible, a faint smudge on the horizon.

'Harmless Hill,' said Edwina Lovely from the bottom step, her eyes following Joe's gaze. 'The fairy folk live beneath it, ruled by their king and queen, Ron and Tania. Secretive folk, keep themselves to themselves as a general rule . . .'

She tossed back her lovely hair and gave a tinkling laugh.

'A little bit like you, Joe the Barbarian. Come . . .' She patted the carpet beside her. 'Sit here next to me and tell me a little bit about yourself.'

Reluctantly, Joe got up from his

seat next to Norbert, who was busy examining the contents of his findy bag, stroking and cooing over each object in turn, and sat down next to Edwina. Perhaps it was her pale skin, cold and clammy to the touch, or her dark-eyed gaze, penetrating and unblinking, or that artificial little laugh of hers— Joe wasn't sure. Whatever the reason, Edwina Lovely made him distinctly uneasy.

'What do you want to know?' said Joe uncertainly.

'Everything,' said Edwina, reaching out and taking Joe's hand in a distinctly clammy grip. 'Such as, where do you come from? And what is your background?' She paused, her eyes growing wide. 'Are you of royal blood?'

'I don't think so,' said Joe, trying to get his hand back. He didn't entirely trust Edwina, and certainly wasn't going to tell her about the lamp-post and the wardrobe and where exactly it was he came from.

'Pity,' said Edwina, tightening her grip and giving him an intense stare. 'I'm a great admirer of royal blood.

Take the kings and queens of Golden Towers, for example—so refined and delicate. Or the Sultans of the South— so full-bodied . . .'

'Yes, well, whatever,' said Joe, tugging harder on his hand.

'Aaah! So you're from Whatever!' said Edwina with a tinkling laugh. 'Twinned with Nowhere!' Her face took on a thoughtful, faraway look. 'It's many years since I had the pleasure of visiting Whatever . . .'

Just then, the stair-carpet gave a shuddering lurch and swerved violently to one side to avoid an immense purple dragon that had flapped slowly into its path. Everyone woke up.

'Watch where you're going!' the dragon huffed smokily, before continuing on its lumbering way.

The stair-carpet gave a little well-pardon-me-for-existing sort of sigh and resumed its flight—but not before Joe had broken free of Edwina's icy grip and scuttled back to Norbert's step.

'Now, what will I find in Goblintown for my findy bag?' the ogre mused, stroking a bath plug on the end of a chain, and returning it to the leather satchel on his lap.

'Edward Gorgeous, with any luck,' said Edwina darkly.

They flew on in silence, the sun sinking low in the sky behind them. Far below, the shadows that streaked the undulating landscape grew longer. They passed over fields and valleys, hills and streams, and a sandpit in which half a dozen trolls with buckets and spades were happily building a sandcastle.

Mile after mile they went. And, as the rippling carpet flew on, its passengers grew drowsy.

Joe closed his eyes, Edwina's lovely head began to nod, while Randalf and Veronica both fell fast asleep, with the budgie on the wizard's shoulder, snuggled up against his beard and snoring. Soon, only Norbert's eyes were open—or rather, *one* of them was. And that was a bit heavy-lidded. The next moment, all three of them blinked with excitement as Norbert caught sight of the fabled walled city, with its glittering towers and smoking chimneys, looming up ahead.

'Goblintown,' he gasped. 'Goblin town, everyone!'

But there was no reply. The others were all fast asleep.

Tiptoeing clumsily to the top step, Norbert eased the staff from Randalf's clutches and raised it above his head. He hit the flying stair-carpet with a resounding *thwack*, sending a cloud of dust up into the air.

'Nice snuggly-wuggly rug,' he boomed in his politest voice. 'Land!'

He thwacked it a second time.

The carpet gave an ouch-that-hurt! kind of sigh and hurtled down towards the ground in a spiralling dive.

'What the . . . ?' shrieked Randalf, waking up and gripping the sides of the carpet in terror.

'Whoooaah!' Joe cried out.

'Waaaah!' screeched Edwina.

The carpet came to a shuddering halt inches from the ground, hovered for a moment, then flipped over, sending its passengers sprawling in the dust. With a that'll-teach-you sigh, it rolled itself up tightly and propped itself against a wall.

'Norbert!' Randalf stormed as he climbed shakily to his feet. 'Give me that staff at once! What were you thinking of?'

'Sorry, sir,' said Norbert tearfully. 'You were all sleeping so peacefully, I didn't want to disturb you.'

'Well, you've certainly disturbed us now!' snapped Randalf. 'Joe? Are you all right? And how about you, Edwina? Here, let me help you up.'

'I'm fine, wizard,' said Edwina testily, brushing the dust from her lovely dress. 'No thanks to Numbutt here.'

'Sorry,' said Norbert, the tears welling up in his triple eyes.

'It's all right,' said Joe, patting the ogre on the back. 'No harm done. And look, we've landed in the perfect place.' He pointed at the building that the rolled-up stair-carpet was leaning against. Like all the buildings of Goblintown, it was tall and tottering, but this one also had a small wooden sign above the door which read, *Brinsley Blowfly's B & B—8th Floor.*

'Perhaps we could get a bed for the night,' Joe suggested.

'Good idea,' said Randalf. 'I'm absolutely exhausted. What I need is a good night's sleep.'

'To go with the good *day's* sleep you've just had,' said Veronica.

'Shut up, Veronica!' said Randalf, picking up the stair-carpet and pushing open the door.

He stepped inside. The others followed, and together they climbed a rickety flight of stairs. Then another. And another. Then a ladder. Then a longer ladder. Then another three flights of stairs, until they came to a low wooden door with *Brinsley Blowfly's B & B* scrawled on it in red crayon.

'This looks like the place,' said Randalf.

'How can you tell?' said Veronica sarcastically.

Randalf reached into his robes and pulled out a small, misshapen silver coin. 'My last pipsqueak,' he said. 'Should be enough for a room for the night—but we can't expect a bed or breakfast.'

Joe frowned. 'So, what does the *B &
B* stand for?'

'Bananas and Broccoli, of course,'
said Randalf. 'To stuff in your ears if
the snoring gets too loud.'

'Silly me,' Joe sighed. 'I should have
guessed.'

Randalf raised his staff and rapped
on the door, which was opened
immediately by a small grubby-looking

goblin.

'What do you want?' he mumbled.

'We seek shelter for the night, my good fellow,' said Randalf cheerily, waving the silver pipsqueak under the goblin's nose. 'Show us the finest accommodation this esteemed establishment has to offer.'

'So you want a room?' said the goblin.

'Indeed we do,' said Randalf.

'Follow me then.'

At the end of a dingy corridor that smelled of old socks and even older underwear, the goblin showed them into a low-ceilinged attic. There was a heap of straw on the floor covered with a sheet, and a threadbare blanket folded beside it. In one corner of the room was a wooden bowl filled with brown-flecked bananas and sprigs of wilting broccoli.

'We'll take it!' said Randalf, handing over the silver pipsqueak.

'Please yourself,' shrugged the goblin. He pocketed the coin and left.

What a dump, thought Joe, looking around the room.

The others didn't seem to notice. Edwina Lovely removed her cloak, spread it on the floor beneath the small attic window and sat down daintily upon it. Norbert plumped up the straw, smoothed out the sheet and laid the blanket over it.

'Your bed's ready for you, sir,' he announced. 'And you, Joe. I'm happy on the floor.'

'Pardon?' said Randalf, who had stuffed a peeled banana in one ear and a sprig of broccoli in the other. 'Ah, I see my bed's ready. Good night, everyone.'

The wizard flopped on to the straw, pulled his hat down over his eyes and started snoring. On the brim, Veronica put her head under her wing. Norbert rummaged in his findy bag, drew out a ragdoll and snuggled it against his cheek as he curled up on the floorboards.

'Good night, Angela,' he cooed, cuddling the ragdoll and closing his triple eyes.

Joe lay down. The straw beneath the sheet felt prickly, but at least it was better than the hard floorboards. Despite the gloom, he was uncomfortably aware of Edwina Lovely, who was still sitting beneath the window, gazing up at the two moons of Muddle Earth which had risen that night. The third was nowhere to be seen.

'Sweet dreams, Joe the Barbarian,' she whispered sweetly.

Joe closed his eyes. Goblintown, he thought. It hadn't changed a jot since the last time he was here. It was still noisy, smelly and overcrowded, and as for the hotel rooms . . .

Randalf was snoring thunderously, and Joe was almost tempted to stuff some of the bananas and broccoli into his own ears. But he was too weary to bother. Despite everything, he must have drifted off to sleep, for some time later something woke him. He opened his eyes and as they became accustomed to the gloom he saw that the attic window was ajar, and Edwina Lovely was nowhere to be seen.

Odd, he thought, and fell asleep again.

'Wakey-wakey, everyone!'

It was Edwina. She looked lovely. Her hair was glossy, her cheeks were rosy and her eyes sparkled.

'It's time to find this goblin, Smutley,' she announced, 'and get him to tell us everything he knows about Edward and his gang . . .'

'Why are you so sure it was Edward who stole the Goblet of Porridge anyway?' said Joe. 'Edward just doesn't strike me as the goblet-stealing type.'

Edwina glared at him. 'If you knew Edward the way I know Edward, you'd understand he's capable of *anything*.' She reached down and pulled the

60

banana out of Randalf's ear. 'Wake up, wizard!' she shouted. 'And let's go and find Smutley.'

'Three and fourpence, and go easy on the jam . . .' said Randalf, sitting bolt upright. 'Where am I?'

'You're in a rundown flophouse in Goblintown being bossed about by a little madam,' said Veronica, *that's* where.'

'Control your parrot, wizard,' snapped Edwina, turning on her heel and marching out of the room. 'Come *on!*' her voice echoed from the corridor.

'You heard her,' said Randalf, climbing to his feet. 'To Grubley's Discount Garment Store!'

Five minutes later, they were striding through the streets of Goblintown. Randalf was in front, staff under one arm and rolled-up carpet under the other, being urged on by a determined-looking Edwina Lovely. Joe followed, with Norbert lagging behind as he scanned the stalls and shopfronts, his hand hovering over the findy bag at his side. Veronica fluttered overhead, muttering under her breath and giving Edwina filthy looks.

'There it is,' said Randalf, stopping in front of a modest tower made up of four clothes shops, one on top of the other. 'Follow me.'

Here we go again, Joe thought as they marched through *Unction's Upmarket Outfitters*, climbed the stairs to *Mingletrip's Middle-of-the-Road Emporium*, took a spiral staircase to *Drool's Downmarket Depot*, and finally braved a flimsy ladder to *Grubley's Discount Garment Store*, where they were greeted by a smartly dressed shop assistant.

'Greetings, gentlemen, lady, budgie,' he said, nodding at each of them in turn and leading them inside the clothing store. 'The name's Smink. How might I facilitate your garment-purchasing needs this fabulous morning? A new gown for sir here?' he said, plucking a shimmering red cape trimmed with sequinned stars from a rail and handing it to Randalf. 'And a hat, perhaps,' he said, removing Randalf's pointy hat.

Veronica hopped on to Joe's shoulder with an indignant chirrup.

Smink placed a huge furry trilby on Randalf's head and steered him towards the mirror. 'And would sir like a tie to go with that? Kipper tie? Eel tie? Herring tie, knitted or unknitted? Halibut cravat? Haddock bow-tie? Oh, sir would look *marvellous* in a haddock bow-tie, if you don't mind me saying so.'

'Actually . . .' Randalf began.

'We're looking for Smutley,' Edwina butted in.

'What's he been up to now?' came a gruff voice, and a grim-faced goblin appeared from behind a rack of blouses. 'No, don't tell me, Randalf, not more exploding gas-frogs! Or have you caught him whittling in the staff room again? If I've told him once, I've told him a thousand times . . .'

'No, no, no, Grubbers,' said Randalf. 'He hasn't done anything wrong. We just want a word with him.' He frowned. 'Is he here?'

'It's "Mister Grubley" to you,' said Grubley, and his eyes narrowed as he

63

noticed the cape and hat Randalf was wearing. 'And are you intending to buy those?'

'They do suit you, sir,' said Smink smarmily.

'OK, Smink, that'll do,' said Grubley, removing the fur trilby from Randalf's head. 'If I know Randalf here, he hasn't got two muckles to rub together.' He took the cape. 'If you want Smutley, you'll find him in Ladies Underwear upstairs.'

They climbed a rope ladder that went up through a hole in the ceiling and found themselves in a small, cramped room full of boxes and crates and bowed racks laden with frilly undergarments. Smutley was kneeling on the floor, a clipboard in one hand and a pencil in the other, busily

ticking off items he was pulling from a large cardboard box.

'Two dozen *Mimi Moo-Moo* baggy-bottom bloomers,' he said, and put a tick next to the order.

'Check. Three dozen pairs of *Twinkletoe* sparkle-tights, with reinforced gussets. Check. Six dozen *Big Bessie* feather-trimmed nighties ...'

'Smutley?' said Randalf.

The goblin spun round. 'Headmaster?' he said, blushing a shade of red that matched the *Big Bessie* feather-trimmed nighties. 'What are you doing here? It's the school holidays, isn't it?'

He noticed Joe standing beside Randalf, and hid the nightie he was holding behind his back.

'Joe the Barbarian,' he said. 'Just helping out my dad with a spot of stocktaking,' he explained.

'And very nice stock it is too,' said Norbert. 'Lovely feathers ...'

'When did you last see Edward Gorgeous?' Edwina interrupted, her lovely eyes flashing. 'He's your team-mate. You're not hiding him, are you?'

'Hiding him? Why would I do that?' said Smutley with a shrug. 'For your information, I've never liked him. Far too full of himself, if you ask me.'

'These really are quite fetching,' said Randalf, holding up a pair of the *Mimi Moo-Moo* baggy-bottom bloomers. 'I particularly like the sparkly cow jumping over the glittery moon on the back.'

'And judging by the size of them,' said Veronica, 'they might even fit you.'

'For crying out loud!' Edwina Lovely said. 'Smutley, when did you last see Edward Gorgeous?'

Smutley scratched his head. 'Last time I saw him, he and your sister— Ella, is it?'

Joe nodded.

'The pair of them were slipping out of the school gates on the back of that battlecat. I thought it was a bit odd at the time, seeing as how we were about to be presented with the Goblet of Porridge. Percy and I had just nipped off to change our shirts. We were hurrying back when Ella and

Edward passed us on the battlecat. Percy was behind me, and I looked round to see Edward lean down and whisper in his ear. I didn't want to miss the presentation so I barged my way through the crowd to the tent, and you know the rest.

'What did Edward whisper?' asked Joe.

'I dunno,' said Smutley with a shrug. 'You'll have to ask Percy that.'

'The troll!' Edwina Lovely exclaimed. 'You know what this means, don't you, wizard? We must go to Trollbridge.'

Randalf put down the baggy-bottomed bloomers and sighed. 'Must we?'

'If you wish to recover the Goblet of Porridge,' said Edwina sweetly.

Randalf shrugged. He laid the roll of carpet down on the floor and tapped it with his staff.

'O floor covering of supreme quality and superlative weave,' he said. 'If you'd be so good as to unroll.'

The stair-carpet obeyed.

'Climb aboard, everyone,' said

Randalf. 'Not you, Smutley. The stair-carpet's quite full enough, thank you.' He tapped the flying carpet a second time. 'Take us to Trollbridge, O tufted transport of delight.'

Moments later, they were sweeping out through one of the narrow windows of the Discount Garment Store, and soaring up into the air. Before long, Goblintown was no more than a faint odour on the wind as the flying stair-carpet carried them across Muddle Earth towards Trollbridge.

Randalf, Joe and Edwina were sitting on their usual steps. Norbert was not. Randalf had just caught him red-handed—and redder-faced—pulling a *Big Bessie* feather-trimmed nightie out of his findy bag, and sent him straight to the naughty step right at the bottom of the carpet, where he would have time to think about just what a naughty thing he'd done.

'I knew it was wrong to take it, Joe,' said Norbert shamefacedly, 'but I just couldn't resist those snuggly feathers.'

But Joe wasn't listening. He was staring at Edwina Lovely, who, with her rosy cheeks and sparkling eyes, was looking lovelier than ever.

'Edwina?' he said.

'Yes, Joe?' she said, turning towards him and flashing him a lovely smile.

'Where did you go last night?'

'Go?' she said. 'I . . . I don't know what you're talking about?'

'I woke up,' said Joe. 'And when I looked over, you weren't there . . . And the window was open.'

'Oh, Joe, you silly barbarian, you must have been dreaming,' she said, and laughed that tinkly laugh of hers. 'I didn't go anywhere.'

It was market day in Trollbridge. In fact, every day was market day in Trollbridge.

As usual, trolls were coming from far and wide, from the turnip patches, the swede fields and the mangelwurzel plots which lined the banks of the Enchanted River. Pushing their rickety wheelbarrows piled high with extravagantly large root vegetables, the trolls raised their voices in happy song as they trundled towards the great arched bridge.

Ten fat turnips sitting on the bridge,
Ten fat turnips sitting on the bridge,
And if one fat turnip should accidently
     slip,
There'll be ... umm ... errrm ...

Ten fat swedes sitting on the bridge,
Ten fat swedes sitting on the bridge,
And if one fat swede should accidently
*   slip,*

There'll be . . . umm . . . errrm . . .
Ten fat mangelwurzels sitting on the
*   bridge,*
Ten fat mangelwurzels sitting on the
*   bridge . . .*

Already on the crowded bridge, the market stalls and benches groaned beneath the weight of pumpkins, parsnips, cauliflowers, cabbages and purple-spotted potatoes of unfeasible size. Matrons in straw bonnets resembling buckets and watering cans mingled with troll maidens with beribboned plaits braided with marrow flowers. Stallholders in capacious aprons and impressive corduroy breeches juggled with knobbly vegetables and called out their wares.

'Sweetest sugar beets, two muckles a basket!'

'Finest potatoes, a pipsqueak a sack.'

'Amusing-shaped carrots, ten groats

72

a snigger!'

Just another market day in Trollbridge. The sun was shining, birds were singing, buckets of manure were gently steaming . . .

'Help! Help! Help!' The cries from beneath the bridge grew louder and more desperate. 'For pity's sake, HELP!'

'Just take Norbert's hand, Randalf,' said Joe, 'and stop making such a fuss.'

'Shan't!' said Randalf. 'It's his fault we got dumped in the river in the first place. How many times do I have to tell you? Don't land the carpet on your own . . .'

'Sorry, sir,' Norbert sobbed. 'I forgot.'

'That's all very well, Norbert,' said Randalf, who was sitting waist-deep in the gently flowing waters of the Enchanted River, his soggy pointy hat drooping, 'but look at the carpet. It's ruined.'

The flying stair-carpet was lying in a sodden heap on the riverbank, where Joe, Edwina and Norbert had hauled it. They too were soaking wet. From overhead came a smug chirp as

Veronica fluttered down and landed on Joe's shoulder.

'Looks like the naughty step for you again, Norbert,' she giggled. 'If that thing ever flies again.'

'Stand up, Wizard,' said Edwina, dripping wet but still lovely. 'We haven't got time for this. Let's get on to the bridge and find that troll, Percy.'

Randalf climbed meekly to his feet and waded to the riverbank with as much dignity as he could muster. Edwina turned on her heel and marched up the path towards the magnificent gate-towers of Trollbridge. The others followed, with Norbert bringing up the rear, a crumpled mass of dripping carpet cradled in his arms. They approached the large wooden gateway that led on to the bridge, where a portly troll in patched dungarees was sitting on a three-legged stool. He put out a hand.

'Troll toll,' he said. 'Pay up.'

'Of course,' said Randalf, nodding. He made a great show of going through his pockets. 'Dear, dear,' he said at last. 'I seem to have spent my

last pipsqueak. Edwina, I don't suppose
. . .'

'Like Queen Susan,' she said
snootily, 'I never carry money.'

Randalf sighed. 'Norbert?' he said.

'I've got that I.O.U. you gave me,'
said the ogre, pulling a soggy piece
of paper from his pocket. 'But the
invisible ink seems to have been
washed off.'

'Ah, yes. Well, never mind . . .' he
said. 'How about you, Joe?'

Joe looked in his own pockets.
He pulled out a laminated bus-
pass, a packet of chewing gum and a
rusty washer. The troll seized the
dripping objects.

'That'll do nicely,'
he said. 'I won't
charge you for the
parrot.'

'Budgerigar, *if* you don't mind,' said Veronica stiffly.

The troll heaved himself up off his stool, plodded across to the gate and pushed it open. 'Welcome to Trollbridge,' he said cheerfully, as Randalf, Norbert, Edwina and Joe filed past.

'Parrot indeed!' muttered Veronica as she fluttered down on to Randalf's hat. 'Does he look like a pirate?'

The gate slammed shut behind them.

'Trollbridge!' said Randalf, looking down at a pile of rotten cabbage leaves. 'The city that never sweeps.' He stepped daintily over the cabbage leaves, and into a dollop of manure.

'I see what you mean,' said Edwina, wrinkling her lovely nose. 'Out of the way! Wizard on important business!'

She barged her way through the bustling crowd. It parted before her, the trolls giving the lovely stranger in the damp dress puzzled looks.

'Where do we find this Percy Throwback of yours?' Edwina called to Randalf over her shoulder.

'Percy Throwback?' said a hefty troll

matron in a raffia bonnet shaped like a flowerpot. 'Why, that's old Nodding Ned and Lazy Susan's lad.' She shifted her trug of scallions from one arm to the other and gave Edwina a snaggle-tusked smile. 'They live under number 25, Southside Archway.' She pointed up ahead. 'First right after the marrow stall. You can't miss it.'

Edwina strode off.

'Thank you,' said Joe politely, and hurried after her, followed by Randalf and Norbert.

They reached a large trestle-table with a striped awning flapping above it, where a troll in a smock was busy polishing marrows. To the right of it, embedded in the cobblestones that ran along the balustrade of the bridge, were row upon row of numbered trapdoors.

'Here it is,' Edwina announced, briskly stamping her foot on a green trapdoor with the number 25 painted on it, and stepping back.

From below them came a gruff voice. 'If that's another one of those billy goats, tell him we're not interested.'

A moment later, the trapdoor opened and Percy's head appeared. He stared up at Edwina.

'Do I know you?' he said.

'Never mind that,' said Edwina, fixing him with a penetrating stare. 'I have good reason to be believe that you and that criminal, Edward Gorgeous, are in cahoots . . .'

'In cahoots? I'm not in cahoots. I'm in Trollbridge,' said Percy, perplexed. 'And I don't know where Edward Gorgeous is.'

He noticed the others, who had just caught up with Edwina and were now standing round the trapdoor.

'Headmaster?' Percy said. 'Joe!' He stepped up on to the bridge and shook Joe's hand delightedly. 'That was some broomball match!' he exclaimed. 'We really showed that snooty Golden Towers lot a thing or two. Pity about the Goblet of Porridge though . . .'

'Aha!' said Edwina. 'What exactly can you tell us about the goblet's disappearance? It was Edward, wasn't it? *He* stole it. Didn't he? Come on, admit it.'

'Edward?' Percy shook his head. 'I don't think so. I was just coming back from changing my shirt when Edward and Ella came riding past on a battlecat, and they certainly didn't have the Goblet of Porridge with them. I asked them where they were going and Edward said nowhere . . .'

'Nowhere,' Edwina breathed.

'Very interesting,' said Randalf, tugging at his beard. 'So it *must* have been the jeer-leaders who stole the Goblet of Porridge . . .'

'Percy? Percy! Who is it?'

Two more heads appeared at the trapdoor.

'Mum, Dad,' said Percy excitedly as his parents stepped up on to the bridge, 'it's my headmaster. And my friend Joe from school. And this is Norbert, who does the dinners, and Veronica, the headmaster's secretary bird.'

'Very pleased to make your acquaintance,' said Nodding Ned, nodding.

'Any friends of Percy's are always welcome here,' said Lazy Susan. 'Oh, my goodness! What have you done to

that carpet?' she said, her gaze falling on the soggy stair-carpet in Norbert's arms. 'Here, give it to me. Let me hang it up for you.' She took the carpet from Norbert, carried it across to the side of the bridge and hung it over the balustrade. 'It'll be dry in no time.'

'Well, we're not going anywhere until it is,' said Randalf.

'Then you must join us for a spot of lunch,' said Lazy Susan. 'I've got a lovely mangelwurzel tart with turnip custard and all the trimmings.'

Nodding Ned nodded.

'And you're all very welcome,' said Percy. 'Even what's-her-name.' He frowned. 'Where is she?'

Everyone looked around, but Edwina Lovely was nowhere to be seen.

'Too sneaky by half, that one,' said Veronica.

'She calls me Numbutt,' said Norbert.

'She gives me the creeps,' said Joe.

'I know what you mean,' said Randalf. 'And she's a little too bossy for my liking.' He rubbed his tummy and turned to Lazy Susan. '*Mangelwurzel* tart, did you say? With turnip custard and *all* the trimmings?'

Nodding Ned nodded enthusiastically.

After what could only be described as a veritable banquet of root vegetables of every shape, size and description, served by their generous hostess on an enormous revolving table, Joe was feeling rather sick. And it wasn't just the food . . .

Although his big sister had run off with a barbarian to goodness knows where on the back of a battlecat, at least Joe now knew that they weren't part of this gang Edwina had gone on about. According to Percy, those strange jeer-leaders were acting on their own in stealing the goblet. Edwina had been wrong to accuse Edward of being their leader.

What did she have against the handsome barbarian anyway? Joe wondered.

The thing was, now that Edwina had run off, he couldn't even ask her. The Goblet of Porridge, the jeer-leaders, Edward, his sister Ella, Edwina—*all* of them had disappeared. It made his head swim and his tummy gurgle. And the food wasn't helping . . .

The mangelwurzel tart looked like

a cowpat and tasted of mud, while the turnip custard smelled of old wellington boots. As for the trimmings, these turned out to be various jellies in the shape of vegetables that wobbled to and fro as the table slowly turned. Joe took one mouthful of the Brussels sprout jelly and immediately regretted it.

The others had no such misgivings. Randalf and Norbert joined in with the Throwback family with gusto. Meanwhile, Veronica hopped around the table pecking contentedly at pumpkin seeds and pastry crumbs.

'If you'll excuse me,' said Joe, 'I think I need a little bit of fresh air.'

'Excellent idea,' said Randalf, sitting back and patting his mouth with a napkin. 'I think I'll join you. See how the flying carpet's coming along. There's no time to waste. We've still got that goblet to find. Now, where could those jeer-leaders have got to? We've got some serious detective work to do!' He got up from the table. 'Norbert, put down that spoon. And Veronica, hop on to my hat.'

'Your word is my command, Fatso,' said Veronica sarcastically, landing on the brim of his pointy hat.

'Thank you so much,' said Norbert to Lazy Susan. 'That turnip custard was delicious. It tasted just like wellington boots. You must let me have the recipe.'

Randalf shook hands with Nodding Ned, who nodded, and patted Percy on the head. 'See you back at Stinkyhogs next term.'

And with that, they left the Throwbacks' cosy cabin and stepped back on to the bustling bridge. Joe closed the trapdoor of number 25 and followed Norbert and Randalf over to the balustrade, where Lazy Susan had hung the carpet to dry. A short, wiry goblin with a long, thin, drooping moustache was sitting a little way off, his legs dangling over the side of the bridge as he stared glumly at the water below. Lost in thought, he didn't look up as Randalf prodded the soggy carpet with his staff.

'Still a little damp,' he observed, 'but that soak in the Enchanted River has brought out its colours beautifully.'

Joe looked at the carpet. The wizard was right. The once drab brown stair-carpet was now a rich shade of blue, with an intricate border of interwoven leaves, fruits and flowers in an array of exquisite colours.

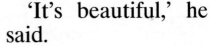
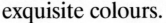

'It's beautiful,' he said.

'Thank you,' whispered the carpet in a small, breathy voice.

'You can talk!' said Joe in surprise.

'That's all we need,' chirped Veronica. 'A talking stair-carpet.'

'Yes,' muttered Randalf to himself. 'Budgies, carpets . . . Whatever next?'

'Thank you, O great magician of large yet dainty feet,' whispered the stair-carpet, 'for your great wisdom in dunking me in the waters of yonder river, thereby washing away all those years of dust and grime. Why, I feel

86

like a completely new carpet—fresh, fragrant and so, so pretty . . . *Tra-la-la-la-la-la* . . .'

'Oh, great,' said Veronica sarcastically. 'A talking, *singing* stair-carpet.'

'*Tra-la-la* . . .' The carpet fell abruptly quiet. 'I don't *believe* it,' it whispered in a small, outraged voice. 'I'd know those feet anywhere!'

It rose a couple of inches from the balustrade and hovered in mid-air, quivering with indignation. Joe, Randalf and Norbert turned and, for the first time, noticed the weedy-looking goblin sitting with his legs dangling down over the side of the bridge. The goblin looked up, his mournful expression changing to one of surprise.

'Randalf? Randalf, is that you?' said the goblin.

Randalf frowned. 'Do I know you?' he said uncertainly.

'Of course you do,' said the goblin. 'Isn't my

voice familiar?'

'Horned Baron!' exclaimed Randalf. 'I didn't recognize you without your horned helmet!' He strode across to him, his hand outstretched. 'How *are* you, my dear chap?'

The Horned Baron's face slumped as he stared down at his dangling feet, the waters of the Enchanted River flowing far beneath.

'Not so good,' he said.

Behind him, Joe heard the carpet harrumph. 'Serves him right for using me as a stair-carpet in his rotten old castle for all those years,' it complained. 'He treated me like a doormat and walked all over me,' it whispered bitterly.

The Horned Baron didn't seem to hear it. His bony body began to shake. His thin moustache trembled and his eyes welled up with tears.

'When I hung up my horned helmet and stepped down from the throne to begin my new life with Fifi, I'd never been so happy. With our beautiful little trapdoor cottage, a turnip patch of our very own and the best humorously shaped vegetable stall in the whole of Trollbridge, who wouldn't be happy? Oh, but now it's all ruined.'

'It is?' said Randalf.

'Utterly,' the Horned Baron said bleakly, and wiped his nose on a grubby handkerchief. 'For Fifi's heart has been stolen by another.'

'It has?' said Randalf.

'Yes!' said the Horned Baron, reaching into his smock and pulling out a dog-eared letter. He flourished it theatrically. 'I have the proof here in my hand. I intercepted the post-elf. *'Dearest Hrothgar,'* he read out in a tearful voice, *'my hero, my life-saver, I'll bring everything you asked for, plus a little something of my own. I want this to be really special.* Look!' he said, waving the letter under Randalf's nose. 'She even underlined the *really special* bit!'

'She did?' said Randalf.

'And there's more!' the Horned Baron wailed. *'I'll see you at your place at the usual time. And remember, on no account is Walter to learn of this! With thanks, love and kisses, Fifi.* Thanks!' the baron moaned. 'Love!' he groaned.

89

'*Kisses!*' He buried his head in his hands. 'I've *lost* her!'

'I'm sure it's not as bad as you think,' said Randalf, patting the Horned Baron on the shoulder.

'It is. It *is* . . .' insisted the Horned Baron miserably. 'Hrothgar! That's a barbarian name. What if he's tall and dark and handsome?'

'Looks are overrated,' said Randalf.

'And rich. What if he's rich?'

'Money isn't everything,' said Randalf.

'And muscles. Great big muscles . . .'

'But you have brains, Horned Baron,' said Randalf.

'And a helmet! What if he's got the largest and most magnificent horned helmet in all of Muddle Earth?'

'*Aaah,*' said Randalf. 'I see your problem. Still,' he said brightly, taking the Horned Baron by the arm, 'you mustn't do anything silly.'

He helped him down from the balustrade.

'Humph,' whispered the carpet huffily. It rolled itself up tightly and leaned against Joe.

90

Just then, the Horned Baron let out a stifled cry and shrank back behind Norbert. 'Shh,' he hissed urgently. 'It's *her*!'

'Who?' said Norbert.

'Haven't you been listening?' chirruped Veronica as a tall, elegantly dressed troll maiden sashayed over the bridge towards them.

She wore a broad-brimmed hat covered in flowering courgettes and carried a large wicker picnic basket on one arm. She was concentrating so intently on the shopping list she held in her gloved hand that she didn't notice the small group on the bridge as she passed by.

'Has she gone?' whispered the Horned Baron a moment later, and stepped out from behind Norbert.

91

He turned to Randalf. 'Do you know what? I'm almost tempted to put on my horned helmet once more and return to the castle . . .'

'To Stinkyhogs?' Randalf squeaked.

Veronica landed on Joe's shoulder and chirruped in his ear. 'If he does, then Fatso's going to be looking for a new job.'

'O floor-covering of colourful delight, unfurl if you please,' said Randalf. The stair-carpet obeyed. They all jumped aboard, and Randalf tapped the carpet with his staff. 'Follow that troll!'

5

With a mighty roar, the magnificent pink-striped battlecat bounded through the forest. Its muscles rippled beneath its sleek pelt as it swerved this way and that, at one with the sinuous movements of its rider.

The barbarian princess sat back in the saddle and twitched the reins in her black-fingernailed hands. In answer, the battlecat swung to the left and ran full tilt towards a sparkling pool of crystal-clear water. Without hesitating, it sprang from rock to rock across the mirrored surface of the pool. Looking down, the barbarian princess caught the fleeting reflection of a powerful battlecat and its graceful rider.

She tugged on the reins, instantly bringing the battlecat to a halt on a mossy boulder. She leaned forward and examined her reflection.

Ella's eyes widened with astonishment. She hardly recognized herself. Staring back at her was a noble barbarian princess, confident and poised, and in perfect control of an extraordinary mythic beast. It felt wonderful, exhilarating, and so natural. It was as if this person had been inside her all along, but trapped and ignored and struggling to get out.

She sat admiring her reflection for several minutes before the low, impatient growl of her battlecat interrupted her thoughts.

'OK, Pinky, time to head back,' Ella agreed.

She twitched the reins, and the battlecat set off once more through the forest. They bounded down the steep wooded slopes, past the mighty waterfall, its spray forming rainbows in the sunny mountain air, and out across the alpine meadow beyond. Crouching in the lush pasture, head down and loppy ears drooping, a giant battlerabbit was grazing intently on the sweet grass, while its rider sat, arms folded, upon its back.

'Hello, Wayne,' said Ella as she trotted past. 'Just taken Pinky out for his early-morning ride.'

'Oh, hello, Ella,' said Wayne, looking up shyly. 'I've been trying to take Benjamin out for his early-morning hop, though we don't seem to have got very far.'

'Never mind,' said Ella, tickling Pinky between the ears. 'See you later.'

Ella pulled up next to the tents and jumped down from Pinky's back. She removed his bridle, unbuckled the saddle and tickled him under the chin.

'Who's a good pussycat?' she said. 'Time for breakfast.'

Pinky purred and nuzzled against her for a moment, before trotting over to join the other battlecats, who were gathered in a circle around a giant saucer, slurping yak milk.

'Good morning, young Ella,' said Deric the Red, emerging from his yak-skin yurt. 'By the tinkling bells of Olaf the Pixie's boots, you're every inch the barbarian princess!' he exclaimed. 'Why, only last night as we feasted, I

95

was saying to Quentin of the Really Large Spoon how impressed I was with you.' He smiled. 'I think you're ready.'

'Ready?' said Ella excitedly.

'Yes,' said Deric the Red. 'Ready to enter the Great Hall!'

He clapped an arm around her shoulders and led her along the broad path through the alpine meadow, away from the cluster of yak-skin yurts and the contented purrs of the breakfasting battlecats, and towards the magnificent wooden building at the centre of the valley. As they approached, Ella looked up. The Great Hall towered above them, tall and majestic, its onion-domed towers gleaming in the sunlight.

From every nook and cranny, the carved heads of barbarian gods and goddesses stared down. Wotulf the Stormbringer, cheeks puffed out and mouth forming an O, clutched an egg-whisk in one clawed hand. Beside him, Freya the Beardy, her plaited whiskers spreading out like branches of a fir tree, cradled a mixing bowl in the crook of her arm and stirred the cake-mixture inside with a hand in the shape of a wooden spoon. The other gods of Asgard were all there too—Gudrun, Igor, Luptoft and Lokki, Beverley, Bruce, Lionel and Stephen—all clutching their immortal implements of culinary prowess. Even Olaf the Pixie, prancing imp of the afterlife, was represented. Carved in seasoned pine, the tiny bells on his pointy-toed boots had been lovingly depicted, along with his twenty-three little fingers, each one sticky with pancake batter.

Deric the Red strode up to the pillared entrance of the hall, raised a

clenched fist and *tap-tappety-tapped* demurely on one of the two huge black-hinged doors.

'By the eggy whisk of Wotulf the Stormbringer,' he bellowed, 'we seek admittance to the Great Hall!'

From inside came the rasp of heavy iron bolts being drawn back and the jangle of chains being removed. A key turned, a latch lifted, and the door creaked slowly open. Deric stepped aside and ushered Ella into the hall.

It took a few moments for Ella's eyes to become accustomed to the gloom. Flaming torches cast a dim, flickering light over the vast interior. The black-and-white-tiled floor was strewn with straw, while heavy timbers formed impregnable, windowless walls which rose up to a vaulted roof of joists and beams high overhead, where fruit-cake bats and cookie ravens flitted to and fro.

Ella followed Deric the Red past a vast brass stove, the length of a broomball pitch, which stood against the wall to her right. Its surface was studded with enough hobs and hot-plates to accommodate a hundred pots and pans, while beneath, a row of gleaming doors concealed ovens big enough to bake a hundred cakes at any one time. At the stove, barbarians wearing pinafores and oven gloves were busy at work, stirring batter, beating egg whites and pouring cake-mixture into buttered cake-trays, the feathers on their winged helmets drooping in the heat.

'Greetings, Ella!' called Rulf Son-of-Rulf.

'Welcome to the Great Hall at last,' chuckled Glenda Daughter-of-Glenda.

'Coming through,' said Nigel Nephew-of-Nigel, rushing past with a trayful of steaming chocolate-chip meringues.

'You'll have to excuse Nigel,' said Deric the Red dramatically. 'He's taking part in the teatime challenge.' He took Ella by the arm and steered her away. 'Come with me,' he said.

Beyond the stove, they came to a huge round table. There was a hole in the middle, in which stood a gilded high-backed throne, upholstered with red velvet. Around the outer circumference of the table stood a ring of three-legged stools. And on one of the stools sat a small, fussy-looking individual with white bouffant hair and a neatly trimmed beard.

'That's Quentin of the Really Big Spoon,' Deric the Red whispered to Ella, stopping at the far side of the table. 'He's our cake druid. We'd better wait here . . .'

In front of the cake druid the place was set with a cup and saucer, a teapot, a milk jug and a sugar bowl with winged tongs, all standing on lace doilies. He held a large wooden spoon in his hand, which he raised and waved.

'Let the challenge begin,' he said grandly.

At his words, three big, burly barbarians lumbered over to the table, elbowing and barging into each other in their eagerness to get there first. Forming a disorderly line, they shoved their plates under the cake druid's nose.

'Gentlemen, gentlemen,' Quentin chided them with a wave of his large wooden spoon. 'How many times must I tell you? Presentation is half the battle!'

The barbarians took a step back and looked at Quentin expectantly. The cake druid inspected the cakes on the plates before him. He poured himself a cup of tea, took a sip and placed the cup back on the saucer.

'Well?' said the barbarians, craning their necks forward and trying to trip each other up.

'You can't rush these things,' said Quentin, picking up the first cake.

It was a squashed-looking Victoria sponge. Quentin sniffed it tentatively, then took a cautious bite.

'Somebody's been overdoing the strawberry jam again, hasn't he, Wulfgar?' he said.

He picked up the second cake.

'Rock cake, Gawain? Really? Do you think that's wise?' Quentin rapped it sharply with his big wooden spoon. 'Suitable for target practice rather than teatime, don't you think?'

He turned to Nigel Nephew-of-Nigel's chocolate-chip meringue.

101

'Intriguing,' he said. He picked the meringue up. 'And so light.' He took a bite. 'Mmm, and really not too bad at all. Mind you, it's still far from the standard required in the Big Barbarian Bake-Off. You've got a lot of work to do, young Nigel. Now, clear the table, all of you.'

'Yes, Quentin. Thank you, Quentin,' the three barbarians chorused, and bowed clumsily.

They picked up their plates and tea things and carried them towards the back of the hall. In the flickering shadows, Ella could just make out the towering outline of the biggest pile of washing-up she had ever seen. Plates were piled on plates, dishes stacked on dishes, platters, pots, pans and bowls heaped in tottering towers and staggering steeples that almost defied belief.

'Impressive, isn't it?' said Deric following Ella's gaze. The barbarians added their plates to the mountain of washing-up and headed back to the stove. 'Nobody has done any washing-up since the days of King Marthur,' he added.

'But why?' said Ella.

'Because of *that*,' said Deric, pointing to the far corner of the Great Hall.

A shaft of light cut through the air at an angle from a window high up in the roof and fell upon a golden-handled sword that was embedded in an ancient cake.

'The Sword in the Scone,' said Deric the Red. 'For it is written, he who pulls the sword from the scone shall become the rightful ruler of the Round Kitchen Table—and has to do all the washing-up.'

As Ella watched, a group of barbarians approached the scone. The largest, a fearsome warrior with a big black beard, spat on his palms and rubbed his hands together. He braced himself on powerful legs and, biceps bulging, seized the handle of the sword and . . . gave it a little tug.

With a theatrical sigh, the mighty barbarian released his grip on the sword handle, stood up straight and wiped the back of his hand across his brow.

'It's beaten me,' he groaned, rolling his eyes and staggering backwards.

His fellow warriors exchanged awkward looks. One examined his fingernails, another shuffled his feet, a third turned a shade of deep red.

At the Round Kitchen Table, Quentin the cake druid looked up and sighed.

'It's remarkable how difficult these big strong barbarians have found it to pull a sword out of a crumbly cake,' he said. 'Isn't it, Deric?' he added pointedly.

Deric the Red blushed furiously. 'This is Ella, Cake Druid,' he said, changing the subject. 'The barbarian princess I was telling you about. Brilliant at battle-roaring, superb at swordplay, astounding at axe-throwing, and a natural battlecat-rider. I think she's ready for the ultimate challenge.'

'Baking a cake?' said Quentin, in tones of hushed awe. 'Step forward, my child.'

He rose from the table and picked up his really big spoon.

'Kneel,' the cake druid told her.

Ella did as she was instructed. Quentin reached out and tapped her with his large wooden spoon, first on one shoulder, then on the other, and finally on the top of her head.

'Go forth and bake,' he intoned.

This was easier said than done, Ella soon realized as she set about the business of barbarian baking. She'd never been much good in the kitchen at home, and here in the Great Hall she was no better. Standing at one of the trestle-tables beside the great stove, Ella was really struggling.

Deric had suggested she attempt iced cupcakes, a barbarian favourite. He took her to the recipe cupboard and selected an ancient parchment, dog-eared and spattered with cake-mix.

'The icing can be tricky,' he said, handing her the recipe, 'but for a barbarian princess like you, Ella, it

106

should be a piece of cake!'

The first egg she tried to crack open exploded in her hand. So did the second. And the third. After half a dozen attempts, she had just about enough egg, not to mention shell, to continue the recipe. Next, she mixed sugar and yak butter together with a three-pronged fork until she was covered in sticky grease. When she sifted the flour it billowed up in a white cloud that made her sneeze, and when she added the milk, she knocked over the milk-jug and soaked the front of her dress.

After what seemed like an eternity of whisking and sieving and creaming and stirring, Ella had finally managed to produce a claggy gloop of cupcake mixture. She dolloped it messily into a row of parchment cups set out on a tray, as Deric the Red looked on, frowning.

'How's that?' said Ella uncertainly.

'Yes, well,' said Deric, eyeing the mess, 'I suppose even the most promising barbarian can't be good at everything.' He shook his head. 'You'd better get them into the oven and hope for the best.'

At the huge stove, where barbarians were coming and going with trays bearing cakes of every description, Deric pulled on an oven glove and opened a door. With a heavy sigh, Ella placed her cupcakes inside. Deric slammed the door shut.

'You might as well take your dirty dishes over to the washing-up pile while you're waiting,' he said, striding off.

Ella returned to the trestle-table to find a couple of black-feathered cookie ravens squabbling over her mixing bowl. They were hugely fat birds, with no necks and bloated bodies supported on thin, spindly legs. Their heads were encrusted in so many layers of dried cake-mix that they appeared to be wearing lumpy, biscuit-like helmets. As Ella watched, the cookie ravens buried their heads inside the bowl and scraped at the sides with their stubby beaks.

'Shoo! Shoo, you stupid creatures!' cried Ella irritably, and flapped her hands at the birds.

With raucous cries of what sounded like 'More, more, ever more!' the two ravens took to the wing. Puffing and panting, they flapped with considerable difficulty up to their roosts in the rafters.

Ella stared down disconsolately at the mess on the table. Drifts of flour mingled with heaps of sugar, eggshells floated in pools of spilt milk, and clusters of claggy cutlery lay beside upended measuring jugs and mixing bowls.

'Need some help?' came a familiar voice.

Ella turned. Edward Gorgeous was standing there, his shirt unbuttoned to the waist and a deathly pallor to his handsome face.

'Oh, Edward,' said Ella. 'I really thought I was good at this barbarian princess business. But I never imagined I'd have to master battlecat-riding *and* cake-baking,' she complained sadly.

Edward smiled and swept her up in his arms. 'No good crying over spilt milk,' he said gently. 'I'm sure you'll get the hang of it eventually.'

'Thank you, Edward,' said Ella, cheering up. 'So, while I've been breaking eggs and spilling milk in here, what have you been up to?'

'Nothing much,' said Edward with a shrug of his broad shoulders. 'Just hanging out in the woods.'

He looked more handsome and brooding than ever. Ella trembled in his arms.

'Edward . . .' she began.

'Benjamin! It's my Benjamin!' came a shout.

All eyes turned towards the doors of the Great Hall, which had just swung open. Wayne the Bunnyrider stood in the entrance, his winged helmet askew and straggly moustache trembling with emotion.

'He's in the meadow, lying flat on his back, shaking from ear-tip to tail. It's his thumb! It's been sucked!'

From every corner of the Great Hall came horrified gasps. Ella turned to

Edward, eyes wide.

'I left him for a minute, that was all, happily chewing the grass. And the only other person in the meadow was—' Wayne's eyes darkened as his gaze fell upon Edward Gorgeous— '*him*!'

'Oh, Edward!'

The barbarians closed in around Edward and Ella, brandishing dripping egg-whisks and crumb-flecked cake-forks. With one arm wrapped protectively around Ella's shoulder, Edward turned to confront the mob.

'It wasn't me!' he protested. 'I didn't do it.' He turned to Ella beseechingly. 'You do believe me, don't you?'

Ella returned his gaze, her eyes full of doubt. 'Oh, Edward . . .'

Quentin the cake druid pushed his way through the crowd of glowering barbarians. He pointed at Edward with his really big spoon.

'Seize him!' he ordered. 'And clap him in irons!'

Two burly barbarians dropped their cooking utensils and obeyed. They grabbed Edward Gorgeous by the arms and frogmarched him away.

'Oh, Edward!!' Ella wailed.

Deric the Red appeared at Ella's side, scratching his ginger beard ruefully. Ella turned to him, tears in her eyes.

'I just don't know what to do,' she said. 'I came here with Edward because I thought it would be a wonderful adventure. And it has been—up until now. He's got his problems, but I thought he was getting over them. With my help. But now he's got himself into terrible trouble . . .'

'It's worse than that,' said Deric darkly, as an acrid smell filled the air. 'You've burned your cupcakes.'

'And another thing,' said the Horned Baron, warming to his theme. 'Her voice. Fifi has the most enchanting voice. It was the first thing I noticed about her. I'll never forget that sunny morning. I was a young goblin, footloose and carefree, and taking in the sights of Trollbridge, when I heard the most beautiful voice. It was coming from a turnip patch. I parted the turnip leaves and there, standing in front of me, was a vision of loveliness . . . .'

Perched on Joe's shoulder, Veronica rolled her eyes. 'I'm not sure how much more of this I can take,' she muttered.

'Shh, Veronica, he'll hear you,' Joe whispered.

He was sitting on the fourth step of the stair-carpet as it flew through Trollbridge. Below Joe, Norbert was back on the naughty step, while above, on the top step, Randalf and the Horned Baron sat side by side. The wizard's head was beginning to nod as the baron droned on.

'It was love at first sight! And Fifi felt the same way. But our love was doomed from the start, for I was betrothed to another. Ingrid . . .'

Veronica shuddered.

'That summer in the turnip patch was the most wonderful of my young life, but Ingrid's mother, Gertrude, put a stop to all that. Then years later, I heard that enchanting voice again in *Mucky Maud's Custard Club* in Goblintown. It was Fifi, and I knew I couldn't lose her a second time. That's why I left Ingrid, the castle and ruling Muddle Earth behind, and ran away with Fifi –' he put his head in his hands and sobbed—'and now she's running away from *me*!'

Joe held on tight as the stair-carpet swerved round a root-vegetable stall and swept over a barrow piled high with pumpkins. Ahead of them, disappearing through the toll gates, was the love of the Horned Baron's life, Fifi the Fair.

'She's getting away,' the Horned Baron cried, nudging Randalf in the ribs. 'Can't this thing go any faster?'

'Never seen those bloomers before in my life . . . What? What?' said Randalf, waking up with a start.

'Faster! Faster!' insisted the Horned Baron.

'Yes, certainly,' said Randalf, gathering his wits and tapping the stair-carpet with his staff. 'If you wouldn't mind, dear carpet.'

'Anything for true love,' it whispered back. 'Despite myself, I found the Horned Baron's story really quite moving.'

It soared up into the air, over the gate-towers of Trollbridge, and out across the swede fields and turnip patches beyond. Below them, Fifi was making her way along a winding path that followed the twists and turns of the Enchanted River. Just after a potato field, she came to a yak-skin yurt that was pitched on the riverbank. As she approached, the tent-flaps were thrown

116

open and a barbarian warrior stepped
out.

He was colossal, his huge shoulders
clad in a black bearskin, his barrel-
chest encased in a chain-mail shirt
and his tree-trunk legs wrapped in
cross-laced fleece to the knee. The sun
played on the enormous helmet on his
head, gleaming on its burnished bronze

surface and glinting on the tips of its magnificent horns.

The Horned Baron turned pale.

With a sweep of one hefty, muscle-bound arm, the barbarian ushered Fifi inside the yak-skin yurt and disappeared after her. The tent-flap dropped back into place.

Up on the stair-carpet, Randalf and the Horned Baron exchanged looks.

'Of course, we could go in there and teach that barbarian a lesson,' said Randalf.

'Errm . . . yes, yes,' said the Horned Baron.

'But perhaps we should listen outside before we go rushing in,' said Randalf.

'Good idea,' said the Horned Baron.

'Scaredy-cats,' Veronica whispered in Joe's ear.

'Lovely stair-carpet,' said Randalf, 'hover above that tent as quietly as you can, if you'd be so kind.'

'Certainly, O great magician,' whispered the carpet, and swooped down towards the yurt.

As they approached the top of the

tent, they heard the sound of voices coming from inside.

'Magnificent!' Fifi's voice rose in excitement. 'Absolutely magnificent!

'Do you really think so?' came a deep, booming barbarian voice. 'You're not just saying that?'

'Oh, no, Hrothgar,' said Fifi breathlessly. 'When I say magnificent, I really mean it. They're so curvy, for a start,' she went on. 'And so deliciously pointy.'

'Yes, they are,' Hrothgar agreed. 'I am rather proud of them.'

'And that's not all,' said Fifi. 'The finish, it's so flawless! I don't know how you manage it!'

'Years of training,' said Hrothgar modestly. 'But it's sweet of you to say so.'

'I could just stand here all day admiring it,' said Fifi. She gave a little laugh. 'But if I did that, Walter would be sure to find out and that would ruin everything! Talking of which, I really must get back home before he misses me . . . Oh, but what's this?'

'It's paint. For your nails,' said

119

Hrothgar smoothly. 'It's all the rage. A barbarian princess called Ella started it. She turned up in Nowhere with black fingernails, and now all the maidens are painting theirs the same colour. I thought you might like it,' he said.

'How very thoughtful of you, Hrothgar,' said Fifi. 'Anyway, I must dash.'

'You heard her, comely carpet of splendour,' hissed Randalf. 'Get us back to Trollbridge at the double.'

They soared off. The Horned Baron looked back over his shoulder as the yurt receded into the distance.

'Black fingernail paint!' the Horned Baron raged. 'Did you hear that? *Black fingernail paint!* Just wait till she gets home! I'll have something to say to her about black fingernail paint—*and* horned helmets!'

'Randalf,' said Joe excitedly, scrambling up to the top step. 'Randalf, that barbarian knows where Ella is.'

'Yes,' said Randalf. 'Nowhere.'

'But she's got to be *somewhere*,' said Joe, confused.

'Nowhere is a place, Joe,' chirruped Veronica from Joe's shoulder. 'It's off the edge of the map, where all those barbarians in nasty winged helmets live.'

'And that's where Ella is?' said Joe. 'We must go there.'

'First things first, Joe,' said Randalf. 'We're searching for the Goblet of Porridge, remember?'

'I know,' said Joe. 'But couldn't we go to Nowhere first to find my big sister? *Please*, Randalf . . .'

'Oh, if you insist.' Randalf sighed. 'But then we search for the jeer-leaders. Is it a deal?'

'It's a deal,' agreed Joe, relieved.

'We'll set off just as soon as we've dropped the Horned Baron at his cottage in Trollbridge,' said Randalf.

'Number 16, Northside Archway,' said the Horned Baron bleakly.

The Horned Baron's cottage was a pleasant little timber cabin hanging from the underside of the bridge beneath a neatly painted trapdoor. It had two bedrooms, one bathroom with a maplewood hot tub and a watering-can shower, and a spacious sitting room with double windows set into the floor, through which the gently flowing waters of the Enchanted River could be seen. Fifi had furnished the cottage tastefully with wheelbarrow chairs upholstered in floral fabrics, and sideboards and cupboards beautifully constructed from antique mangelwurzel crates. It was in one such cupboard that the Horned Baron was frantically rummaging.

'Where *is* it?' he fumed. 'I know it's here somewhere . . .'

Joe watched from one of the wheelbarrow chairs as the contents of the cupboard flew across the room. A bag of assorted marbles. A green muffler with *I Love Trollbridge* stitched into it in red letters. A copper tankard stamped with the name *Mucky Maud's Custard Club*. A rubber duck. A wind-up gas-frog. And a portrait of a humorously shaped turnip labelled *Gertrude* . . .

'Can't we go now?' asked Joe, looking across at Randalf in the other wheelbarrow chair.

Norbert stood behind him, holding the rolled-up carpet.

'The sooner the better,' said Veronica, dodging an old slipper as she flew across the room and landed on Randalf's shoulder.

'We can't leave him like this,' said Randalf. 'Not until Fifi gets home. The poor fellow's clearly distraught . . .'

Just then, from the depths of the cupboard there came a triumphant cry.

'There you are! At last! How I've missed you!' The Horned Baron turned round and stepped from the cupboard, the large horned helmet his butler had returned to him in his arms. He put it on. 'That's better,' he said. 'Now I feel

123

like a ruler again. Powerful. Ruthless. With an iron fist and a heart of stone!'

He strode over to the potting-shed table, pulled up a chintz-covered crate and sat down. He folded his arms and glared up at the trapdoor at the top of the stairs. Moments later, there was the *trip-trap* of approaching footsteps. The trapdoor opened and a billy goat poked its head inside.

'Get out!' bellowed the Horned Baron.

The billy goat's head disappeared and the trapdoor slammed shut.

After a few moments the trapdoor opened again and this time Fifi the Fair stepped through. She descended the stairs, her large picnic basket clutched protectively in her arms.

'I see we've got guests,' she said brightly. 'How lovely.' She paused. 'Why, Walter, you're wearing your helmet. Are you feeling all right?'

The Horned Baron drew himself up to his full height, which was helped by the chintz-covered crate on which he now stood.

'What's in the basket?' he demanded imperiously.

'It's nothing, Walter,' she said. 'I've just been doing a little shopping, that's all.'

'A little shopping, eh?' said the Horned Baron, his eyes glaring from the depths of his horned helmet. He shot out an arm and pointed at the basket. 'Open it!' he commanded.

'Walter,' said Fifi. 'Haven't we forgotten to say *please*?'

'OPEN IT!'

Fifi took a step back. 'I was hoping it would be a surprise,' she said with a rueful smile. 'But since you insist . . .'

'I DO!'

Fifi removed the chequered cloth that covered the basket. She reached inside and removed a cake. It was large, round and covered in flawless icing. With its curling horns of spun sugar and glaze of glistening

125

butterscotch, the cake was a perfect replica of the very helmet the Horned Baron was now wearing. In exquisite piped icing-sugar lettering were the words *HAPPY BIRTHDAY, WALTER*.

There was a long silence, during which the Horned Baron's furiously pointing finger fell to his side.

'Absolutely magnificent . . .' he mumbled sheepishly as he remembered Fifi's words in the yak-skin yurt. 'Flawlessly finished . . . Deliciously pointy . . .'

Fifi reached out with black-fingernailed hands and placed the birthday cake before him. The Horned Baron stared. Fifi caught his gaze and held up her hands.

'Do you like them?' she asked. 'I painted them specially. For you, darling Walter.'

'So you *do* love me,' said the Horned Baron, sitting back down on the chintz-covered crate.

'Of course I do, silly,' said Fifi, smiling. 'You're the only one for me, Walter, you know that. With or without your helmet.'

'But I thought you didn't like me wearing it,' he said meekly.

'Only because of the way you thought you had to behave when you had it on,' she said. 'As I've always told you, Walter, it's not the helmet that's important, it's the goblin inside.'

'So I can wear it again?' he asked eagerly.

'Of course you can,' she replied. 'I know how much you missed your helmet, which is why I had Hrothgar the barbarian cake-maker bake you this birthday cake . . .' She smiled sweetly. 'Shall we?'

The Horned Baron removed the helmet and placed it carefully beside him. He looked up.

'Yes, please!' he said excitedly.

Fifi reached out and gripped him tenderly by the ears.

'*Happy birthday to you*,' she sang sweetly. '*Happy birthday to you. Happy birthday, dear Walter . . .'*

She pushed his face down into the soft, gooey fondant of the helmet-shaped cake.

'Happy birthday to you!'

The Horned Baron let out a long, contented gurgle of delight and sat back up, his face covered in sweet, sticky cake.

'Just like the old days at the Custard Club,' he purred.

'How romantic,' whispered the carpet in Norbert's arms.

The little cloud drifted across the clear blue sky. Catching a gust of wind high above the Perfumed Bog, it enjoyed a pleasant billow in the scented breeze. Drifting on towards the Enchanted Lake, the cloud dallied over the choppy waters, luxuriating in the rising vapours as they plumped it up deliciously. White and fluffy, it moved on, choosing a gust here, a breeze there, an occasional zephyr or two, as it wandered lonely as a cloud—which, since it was indeed a cloud and the sky was remarkably clear, wasn't surprising.

Somewhere over the Musty Mountains, it was browsing the air currents, trying to make up its mind which one to select, when something caught its attention. It was bright and colourful and rippled delightfully as it made its way across the sky. It reminded the cloud of the kites it loved to play with over Goblintown. It broke up into little puffs of pleasure at the memory, before pulling itself together and setting off on a stiff wind towards the beautiful object in the sky ahead.

'Can't think what happened to Edwina,' said Randalf sleepily. 'Still, that's that Golden Towers lot for you. All over you one moment, then drop you like a hot fairy-cake the next.'

'Mmmm, hot fairy-cakes,' said Norbert, from the naughty step. 'Delicious! Though I do like lukewarm goblin-tarts. And I'm very partial to cold ogre-rusks. But snugglemuffins are my favourite, whatever the hotness. You like my snugglemuffins, don't you, Joe?'

'Y . . . Yes,' said Joe distractedly and shivered. 'Is it just me, or is it getting a bit chilly?'

'It's that cloud,' whispered the carpet. 'It's been hovering over us for ages. And every time I change course, it follows.'

'Oh, yes, so it is,' said Randalf,

stifling a yawn. He climbed to his feet and began waving his staff over his head. 'Go away, you silly cloud,' he shouted.

On the brim of Randalf's hat, Veronica pulled her head from under her wing. 'What's all the fuss, Fatso?' she chirped.

'Go on! Shoo!' shouted Randalf.

Above them, the cloud darkened.

'Go *away*,' Randalf insisted, 'you foolish fogbank!'

Rain began to fall.

'Desist, you ridiculous cumulus!'

The cloud grew thunderous and the rain got harder.

'Well done, Fatso,' said Veronica sarcastically. 'Now you've hurt its feelings.'

'Nonsense!' said Randalf, continuing to brandish the staff above his head. 'It's just a stupid cloud. It doesn't have feelings.'

Flashes of lightning fizzed inside the rapidly blackening cloud and a shower of hailstones clattered down.

'Ouch! Ouch! Ouch!' protested the carpet.

Joe and Norbert cowered together on the naughty step while Veronica sought shelter in the folds of Randalf's cloak. The wizard sat back down and pulled his pointy hat down low over his head.

'Stop it, you naughty nimbus!' he squeaked.

There was a flash of lightning and a clap of thunder.

'Oooooaaaaawww!' screeched the carpet, and sped off across the sky at breakneck speed, a twisting trail of pungent smoke unravelling behind it.

The cloud gave chase.

In its panic the carpet had lost its stair shape and was now a long, flapping streak of woven blue. Randalf, Norbert and Joe had tumbled off the back of the carpet and were clinging on for dear life to its tasselled tail.

'Whoah, there!' gasped Randalf. 'Calm yourself, O stair adornment of woven splendour! *Whoah!*'

The stair-carpet slowed down, bunching along its length as it did so until it had regained a semblance of its old shape. Wheezing and puffing,

Randalf was able to clamber back on board once more and resume his seat. Norbert and Joe followed. The ogre eyed the wizard, his triple eyes narrowing.

'Shouldn't *you* be on the naughty step now, sir?' he said.

Veronica popped her head out of the folds of Randalf's cloak. 'Norbert's right, you know,' she said.

'Shut up, Veronica!' said Randalf hotly. He looked round, smoothing down his beard and gathering his cloak around him with as much dignity as he could muster. 'Thank goodness for that,' he said. 'I think we've given that imbecilic cirrus the slip.'

A single snowflake fluttered down and landed on the tip of Veronica's beak.

'Don't speak too soon, Fatso,' she said.

They all looked up. There, hovering above them, was the cloud. It looked bigger and darker and more furious than ever. A second snowflake fluttered delicately down. And a third . . .

133

Then, with a great muffled *whumpf*, the cloud dumped a whole blizzard of snowflakes down on their heads.

'It's freezing!' squealed the carpet, shivering so violently that Joe almost fell off his step again.

Beside him, Norbert was frantically bailing handfuls of snow from the carpet. On the top step, Veronica had disappeared back into Randalf's robes, as the wizard brushed snow from the brim of his pointy hat.

Whumpf!

The blizzard intensified. The snow piled up faster than they could brush it away.

Whumpf!

It settled on their heads and shoulders until they resembled snowmen, and rapidly built up to form drifts that avalanched down the steps.

Whumpf!

'I can't feel my tassels,' moaned the carpet weakly.

It sagged and groaned beneath the weight of snow.

'O car . . . car . . . carpet of de . . . de . . . delight,' Randalf stuttered through chattering teeth. 'Ge . . . Ge . . . Get us ou . . . ou . . . outta here!'

'Prepare for an emergency landing,' whispered the carpet.

'How do we do that?' Joe shouted through the blizzard.

'Just lie down on the naughty step,' replied the carpet.

Joe and Norbert shovelled snow off the naughty step as Randalf slipped and slid down the stairs to join them. They lay down.

'Careful, Fatso!' squawked Veronica. 'Don't squash me!'

The carpet swooped down, rolling itself up tightly as it did so. It fell in a tumbling spiral out of the sky before hitting the ground and bouncing once, twice, three times, and beginning to unfurl. At the centre of the carpet, Joe, Norbert and Randalf were spun round and round. As it finished unrolling, they shot off the end and kept on rolling until, with a *splodge*, they came to an abrupt halt.

High in the sky, the cloud broke up into misty wisps of frustration, before recovering its composure and pulling itself together once more. With a shrug of its fluffy billows, the little cloud drifted huffily away in search of less contrary playmates.

'Gingerbread?' said Joe, sniffing the wall they'd crashed into on landing.

'It's a little stale,' said Norbert critically. 'Not like my snugglemuffins . . .'

'Who's that eating my house?' came a sing-song voice.

Randalf and Joe climbed slowly to their feet and dusted cake crumbs from their shoulders while Norbert took another mouthful of gingerbread wall. Joe looked around. They had crash-landed in a clearing in the middle of Elfwood, and smashed into an extraordinary fairy-tale house.

Its walls were made of gingerbread, with round yellow windows and a

lozenge-shaped door. The pitched roof
was covered with red and black tiles
and edged with twists of translucent
candy guttering. White icing had been
piped over the walls and around the
windows and door, to form intricate
patterns of hearts, diamonds and
squiggly lines, while the garden path
was paved with green, sticky-looking
pastilles.

'Yuk!' exclaimed Norbert, who had
just scooped a dollop of white icing
from a wall and tasted it.

'It's *Dr Greenteeth's Big-Burp*
toothpaste.'

Everyone turned to see Eudora Pinkwhistle standing in the lozenge-shaped doorway.

'Headmaster!' the witch exclaimed, her frown disappearing as her gaze fell on Randalf. 'How nice of you to drop in like this.'

'"Drop" is right!' Veronica's head popped out from the folds of the wizard's cloak. Her scarf was askew and her little bobble hat had slipped down over one eye. She spotted the witch's cat, Slocum, slinking out from the doorway and licking her lips. Veronica's head disappeared again. 'It gets worse and worse,' came her muffled voice from the depths of Randalf's robes.

'Ignore Veronica,' said Randalf. 'It's lovely to see you. We were just on our way to Nowhere on our flying stair-carpet when we experienced a little turbulence . . .'

The stair-carpet, which had rolled itself up and tucked itself quietly under Randalf's arm, gave a little shiver.

'But we mustn't intrude,' he said. 'After all, it is the school holidays. If you'll excuse us, we'll be on our way . . . Norbert! Put down that roof tile!'

'*Burp* . . . Yes, sir. Sorry, sir,' said Norbert, reaching up and pushing the tile back into place. 'It tastes horrid anyway.'

'Really?' said Eudora sternly. 'The elves adore *Menthol Murphy's Liquorice and Aniseed Squares*. But headmaster, I can't let you rush off like this. Come in for a nice cup of tea.'

'If you insist,' Randalf sighed reluctantly.

'Oh, I do, I do, headmaster,' said Eudora, ushering them inside. 'You must tell me all the news from Stinkyhogs. Have you recovered the Goblet of Porridge? Is Roger the Wrinkled still cross with you? When does the new term start—if it *is* going to start, that is? And did I hear you were heading for Nowhere? Why, what a coincidence . . . But I'm forgetting my manners,' she said, 'bombarding you with all these questions. Do sit down and I'll put the kettle on.'

The stale-gingerbread house was far smaller inside than it looked from the outside. Randalf, Norbert and Joe sat bunched together on a lumpy sofa, while behind them Eudora Pinkwhistle fussed about at the tiny stove.

'Ooh, no! Stop it! Oh no! No, no, no, no. Stop it! Stop it! That tickles . . . Ha ha ha ha ha!'

As the kettle came to the boil, Eudora removed it from the stove and poured the steaming water into a brown teapot.

'The water's from the Babbling Brook,' she explained. 'Nice and quiet once it's been boiled.'

She poured cups of tea and handed them round. Then, taking down a cake-tin from an extremely small dresser in the corner, she turned and smiled.

'Fairy-cake, anyone?'

They reached into the cake-tin in turn.

'They're delicious!' Norbert exclaimed, swallowing three of the little cakes in one go.

'Yes, really excellent,' agreed Randalf.

Joe bit into his fairy-cake uncertainly. But despite the witch's stale gingerbread house, he had to admit her fairy-cakes were really very good.

'I'm so glad you like them,' said Eudora, drawing up a small rocking chair and sitting down opposite them. 'I've been practising all holiday. I'm entering the Big Barbarian Bake-Off in Nowhere. So you see, *I'm* going there too!' She frowned. 'Why are you going there anyway? On the trail of the missing goblet, perhaps?'

'Well, yes, sort of,' Joe broke in. 'But it's my sister Ella *I* want to find, and we heard that she's in Nowhere. She ran away with Edward Gorgeous after the broomball match . . .'

'Edward Gorgeous,' said Eudora Pinkwhistle. 'Such a polite young man. A little quiet, certainly, but a pleasure to teach. Don't you agree, headmaster?'

She leaned forward in the small rocking chair until her knees were touching Randalf's. She fluttered her eyelashes.

'So what do you think of my little house, headmaster?' she asked, leaning even closer as she changed the subject. 'Don't you just adore it? I have to admit, I had my doubts about Giggle Glade when I first moved here. My, but you should have seen the state of this place! A dreadful little teddy had been living here in an awful wooden shack. Well, of course I tore it down and started again. Completely transformed it into what you see around you. The elves simply can't get enough of it!' She held out the teapot in one hand and proffered the cake-tin with the other. 'More tea, headmaster? More cake?'

Just then, Slocum leaped up on to Randalf's lap and started sniffing at his cloak. From deep inside the folds of material came a muffled cry of outrage.

'Get that creature away from me!'

Joe gathered a protesting Slocum in his arms and, squeezing past Randalf and Eudora, got up from the sofa. 'Shall I put the cat out?' he said.

'That would be sweet of you,' said Eudora.

Joe crossed to what he took to be the front door and opened it. There, on the other side, was an iron staircase that

led down into a cavernous basement. From the top of the stairs, Joe could see dozens of elves. They were dashing around in circles, chattering in high-pitched elf voices as they kept repeating the questions they'd been asked so that they wouldn't forget them.

'Goggle, goggle, goggle, goggle, goggle . . . How many muckles in a pipsqueak?'

'Goggle, goggle, goggle, goggle, goggle . . . What's the colour of Roger the Wrinkled's beard?'

'Goggle, goggle, goggle, goggle, goggle . . . Who *is* the fairest of them all?'

At the far end of the room, other elves were arriving and leaving through a trapdoor in the ceiling, sliding down a long pole one way and climbing up a dangling rope-ladder the other. At the centre of the room, hovering above the floor at the end of a heavy iron chain, was a large leatherbound volume, the name *Muddlepedia* emblazoned on its spine. One by one, the elves approached the book, riffled through its pages, repeating their questions as they did so, until they came to the answers they were searching for.

'Two and a half . . . goggle, goggle, goggle. Depending on how squeaky the pip is.'

'Pink on Tuesdays . . . goggle, goggle, goggle. White on Wednesdays and soggy at bathtime.'

'Not you . . . goggle, goggle, goggle, Baroness Ingrid.'

Repeating their answers over and over, they turned away and headed for the dangling rope-ladder. In Joe's arms, Slocum squirmed and miaowed excitedly.

'Not that door, young man,' Eudora called from the rocking chair. '*That* one.'

'Sorry,' said Joe, feeling foolish. He closed the door and headed for an identical one opposite and let Slocum out. 'If you don't mind me asking,' he said politely, 'what's going on down in the basement?'

'Oh, it's a little sideline of mine. I call it the Muddle-Wide-Web. And those are my inter-elves.'

'An absolute marvel,' said Randalf, nodding enthusiastically. 'Miss Pinkwhistle gave Stinkyhogs one of her goggle boxes. Ask it any question you like and the inter-elf inside pops out and goes off to find the answer.'

'It runs itself really,' said the witch modestly. 'Elves love dashing about— almost as much as they love stale gingerbread and throat-lozenges. Which reminds me. I must get that cough-candy guttering seen to . . .' She turned to Randalf. 'Do have another fairy-cake, headmaster.'

'Oh, I've had more than enough, thank you, Eudora,' said Randalf, picking up the carpet which was nestling at his feet. 'We really should be on our way, if we're to get to Nowhere by nightfall.'

'You're absolutely right, dear headmaster,' agreed Eudora. 'Dyson! Dyson! Over here, broom. We're leaving this instant.' She opened the front door. 'Slocum! Here, kitty, kitty, kitty . . .'

From the folds of Randalf's cloak came a muffled voice. 'That's it!' it said. 'I'm never coming out now!'

Delia finished buffing her nails and picked up the ornate mirror with its filigree handle and seashell-decorated frame. With her other hand she picked up a pair of curling tongs and delicately applied them to the wispy eyelashes of first one eye, then the other. She blinked seductively.

'Who's a pretty little thing?' she cooed to herself and gave a girlish giggle.

She put down the hand-mirror and curling tongs and reached out for the tray of teacakes. Plump and round, and with criss-cross indentations on the top, the teacakes were cinnamon-scented and speckled with currants, raisins and slices of candied peel. She eyed the dainty cakes appreciatively.

'I'm an artist,' she cooed. 'Mistress

of the meringue, guru of the gateau, diva of the drop scone . . . Those fools! They've never appreciated my genius. But I'll show them!' she exclaimed, her eyelashes fluttering.

She skewered a teacake with a three-pronged toasting fork and held it aloft.

'Now for the finishing touch,' she whispered.

Opening her great purple-scaled jaws wide, she exhaled a dazzling plume of flame, twirling the toasting fork expertly as she did so. Three blinks of a dragon's eye later, her mouth snapped shut.

The teacake was golden-brown with twists of cinnamon-scented steam rising from its toasted centre. Delia the dragon smiled.

'Perfection,' she breathed.

The pink frog crouching on the broad mauve lily-pad let out a little *gribbit* and expanded.

'*Whiffle-piffle! Whiffle-piffle!*' it croaked quietly.

It opened its powder-blue eyes and blinked several times in rapid succession before shutting them tightly again.

'*Whiffle-piffle! Whiffle-pip-pip-pip!*' it croaked, expanding some more. '*Whiff-whiff-whiff-WHIFF!!*'

Its glistening pink body swelled to five times its normal size and its blue eyes bulged open, giving the gas-frog a look of startled surprise.

'*WHIFF-WHIFF-WHIFF . . .*'

BANG!

A cloud of pink gas plumed up and hung for a moment in the perfumed air. Then, with a *plip, plip, plop, plop,* a thousand tiny tadpoles rained down into the bog-pool below.

The now empty lily-pad trembled and began to rise slowly from the surface of the water. Two eyes, a nose, a mouth and chin appeared, followed by a thin, scraggy neck and sloping shoulders. As the lily-pad rose higher a round body supported by thin stilt-like legs emerged, dripping, into the pink-tinged light. Two stick-like arms, as thin as the stilt-like legs, reached up and adjusted the lily-pad hat.

'Greetings, little pongpoles,' the perfumed bog-man said appreciatively in a gurgly, water-down-the-plughole kind of voice.

He reached out a long thin arm and stirred the tiny tadpoles in the water around him affectionately, before turning and plunging his other arm deep into the pool. He felt about in the muddy waters for a moment. Then, with a grunt of effort, he pulled his arm out again. In his hand was a small leather

151

suitcase, lightly crusted with bog-barnacles and trailing fronds of pond-slime.

Swinging the suitcase merrily, he set off, striding on his stilt-like legs through the Perfumed Bog.

'See you later, pink stinky hogs! So long, exploding gas-frogs! Goodbye, little pongpoles!' he burbled in his gurgly, gargly voice. 'Old Peat's off to seek his fame and fortune!'

The sleek battlecat strained at its harness as it pulled the covered chariot over the rolling grassland, past Harmless Hill on one side and, far in the distance, the Sandpit on the other. Seated in the chariot, wearing an impressive horned helmet and bearskin coat, was a hulking barbarian. On the chariot's canvas covering, painted in large black Gothic letters edged in gold, was the name *HROTHGAR the HUNGER SLAYER*, while beneath, in

a small fussy-looking script, were the
words *Barbarian Baker and Peripatetic
Patissier.*

'Whooah there, Sweetfang!'
Hrothgar the Hunger Slayer bade
his battlecat, pulling on the reins and
bringing the chariot to a halt. 'By the
Spooned Hand of Freya the Beardy,
what have we here?'

In the shadow of Harmless Hill,
behind a petal-covered trestle-table,
stood four fairies. They wore black
singlets decorated with white skull
polka dots, tattered black tutus, stripy

153

black-and-white tights and heavy black boots. At their shoulders were translucent gossamer wings that shimmered in the bright sunlight.

'Greetings, barbarian warrior,' said the fairies' leader, who was tall and willowy, with long green hair and a pale complexion. She raised a jug in one hand and a tulip-shaped glass in the other. 'Can we offer you refreshment? Sparkling daisy dew, freshly made. Only a muckle a glass.'

She poured a yellow cordial from the jug into the glass and held it out. Her three companions gathered round. The first had a shock of purple hair, the second a magenta bob, while the third had straggly braids of bleached white. They looked at the barbarian expectantly.

'Don't mind if I do,' said Hrothgar, leaping down from his chariot and flipping a brass coin on to the table. He reached to his belt, unhooked his drinking horn and held it out. 'But I'm a barbarian and we drink only from these.'

The fairy with the green hair

emptied the glass into the drinking horn and topped it up to the brim from the jug. Hrothgar raised it high.

'In true barbarian fashion, I give you this toast,' he announced, his even white teeth flashing in a dazzling grin. 'May your petals glisten as brightly as Olaf the Pixie's twenty-three fingers and your facial hair grow as luxuriantly as Freya the Beardy's!'

The four fairies exchanged looks as the barbarian put the drinking horn to his lips and drained it in one go. He wiped his mouth flamboyantly on the back of his hand.

'That was excell—'

Like a mighty pine tree falling in the mountain forests of Nowhere, the hefty barbarian warrior toppled forward and hit the ground with a resounding thud. Pesticide the flower fairy tossed back her green hair and smiled malevolently.

'Looks like we're in business, girls!'

'Are you sure you wouldn't like to ride up here with me, headmaster?' said Eudora Pinkwhistle. 'For there's room on my broom for two. And broom-riding is so, so exhilarating!'

She hovered above the top step of the flying stair-carpet on her broom, Dyson. Her cat, Slocum, nestled in her lap.

'That's very kind of you, Eudora,' said Randalf sleepily. He yawned. 'But I'm more than happy where I am.'

'So am I,' came a muffled voice from his robes.

Joe and Norbert were sitting side by side halfway down the stair-carpet as they flew high over the Musty Mountains on the way to Nowhere.

'And this is one of my favourites,' Norbert was saying, pointing at a particularly grubby and well-thumbed page of his recipe book. 'Upside-down cake. You make it standing on your head.'

Joe smiled as the ogre turned the page. 'And this is jumping-up-and-down cake. You make it jumping up and down. And this one,' Norbert said,

156

'is cartwheel cake.'

'Don't tell me,' said Joe, and laughed. 'You make it turning cartwheels.'

'No, Joe,' said Norbert, puzzled. 'It's a cake the size of a cartwheel.'

The pair of them ducked down as Eudora Pinkwhistle came swooping over their heads and sped off into the sky ahead. She turned round and waved.

'Catch me if you can, slowcoaches,' she giggled.

The Great Hall of the barbarians of Nowhere towered high above the cluster of yak-skin yurts in the lush alpine meadow. From the forested slopes of the surrounding mountains came the raised voices of barbarians calling words of encouragement.

'Good luck, Nigel!'

'You can do it, my son!'

'Break an egg!'

Nigel Nephew-of-Nigel
steered his battlecat
out of the forest,
across the green
meadow, and stopped
in front of the arched
doorway of the Great
Hall. He leaped from
his steed and strode up
to the formidable black-hinged doors.
He raised a clenched fist and rapped
politely. The doors opened.

'It is I, Nigel Nephew-of-Nigel, here
to claim my place in the Big Barbarian
Bake-Off.'

'Enter, Nigel Nephew-of-Nigel,' said
a voice from the shadows.

Nigel stepped inside and the doors
slammed shut.

High in the sky, there
came the sound of mighty
wingbeats, growing
louder as a purple
dragon emerged from
the clouds overhead
and descended towards
the Great Hall. It
landed in front of the

158

black-hinged doors, reached out a taloned claw and tapped lightly on the wood. The doors opened.

'Hello, dear thing. My name's Delia Dragonbreath and I'm here to enter your marvellous Barbarian Bake-Off.'

'Enter, Delia Dragonbreath,' came the voice from the shadows.

Folding her wings neatly and gathering up the coils of her tail over one arm, she ducked her head and stepped inside. The doors slammed shut.

Just then, what looked like a spinning mauve cartwheel came rolling down the mountain slope and burst out from the trees. It was followed moments later by a tumbling boulder. The two of them bowled across the meadow, past the yurts, and crashed one after the other against the doors of the Great Hall. The boulder unfurled stick-like arms and stilt-like legs and climbed

159

to its feet. It swept up the cartwheeling lily-pad hat and placed it on its head.

The doors opened.

'Peat the Perfumed Bog-Man at your service. I'm here to seek my fame and fortune in this here Barbarian Bake-Off of yours.'

'Enter, Peat the Perfumed Bog-Man,' said the voice.

'Much obliged,' said Peat, loping inside.

The doors slammed shut.

A little while later, a covered chariot pulled by a striped battlecat drew up outside the Great Hall. A tall figure in an impressive-looking horned helmet and a floor-length bearskin coat climbed down from the chariot and tottered over to the doors. It reached out a mittened hand and knocked.

The doors opened.

'*Ahem*,' said a soft, high-pitched voice, which changed suddenly to a low, gruff one. 'It is I, Hrothgar the Hunger Slayer,' the voice growled through a heavy black beard that slipped to one side, only to be pushed back into place by the mittened hand.

'We're here . . . I mean, *I'm* here, to enter the Big Barbarian Bake-Off.'

Two green eyes blinked from the shadows beneath the impressive horned helmet.

'Enter, Hrothgar the Hunger Slayer!' the voice replied.

Arms outstretched and helmet wobbling, the barbarian lurched inside. The doors slammed shut.

Ten minutes came and went. Barbarians on battlecats emerged from the surrounding forest and made their way to their tents. Wood was chopped and cooking fires were lit. Kettles were boiled, teapots were filled and sandwiches passed around, while at their giant saucer, battlecats gathered to slurp stiltmouse milk.

From high over the treetops a witch on a broom appeared and circled the onion towers of the Great Hall, before swooping down to land at the black-hinged doors. She rapped on them briskly.

The doors opened.

'Miss Eudora Pinkwhistle of Ginger Gables, Giggle Glade. I wish to enter your Big Barbarian Bake-Off.'

'Enter, Miss Eudora Pinkwhistle,' said the shadowy voice.

With Dyson under her arm, she bustled inside the Great Hall and the doors slammed shut behind her. As they did so, a stair-carpet came into view. It descended rapidly out of the sky and came to a hovering halt a few inches above the lush meadow-grass in front of the yak-skin yurts.

Randalf, Norbert and Joe stepped from the stair-carpet.

'Well done, dear carpet of incomparable comfort,' said Randalf.

'Yes,' said Veronica, appearing from the folds of his cloak, 'you certainly gave that old witch and her nasty cat the slip.'

'It's so nice to be appreciated,' whispered the carpet, rolling itself up and snuggling under the wizard's arm.

Breaking away from the others, Joe ran up to a barbarian who had just emerged from a tent.

'Excuse me,' he said, 'but have you seen a tall barbarian princess? Fair hair. Black fingernails. Can be a bit sulky. Her name's Ella, and she's travelling with a boy called Edward . . .'

'By the Whiskers of Miffy the Magnificent!' exclaimed the red-bearded barbarian. 'But of course I have. She's one of my best pupils. The name's Deric the Red, by the way.'

He shot out a big meaty hand. Joe shook it.

'I'm Joe,' he said. 'Ella's younger brother.'

'Pleased to make your acquaintance, Joe Brother-of-Ella,' said Deric the Red warmly. His expression darkened. 'I'm afraid I've got some bad news. Edward and Ella have been clapped in irons.'

'Clapped in irons!' Joe exclaimed.

'Clapped in irons?' repeated Randalf, arriving at Joe's side.

'Sounds serious,' said Norbert behind them.

'It is,' confirmed Deric, nodding gravely. 'When Edward was accused of

164

thumbsucking, Ella lost her temper with our cake druid. She tipped a bowl of pancake batter over his head, and that's about as serious as it can get.'

'So where exactly are they now?' said Joe.

The barbarian turned and pointed at the towering, onion-domed building at the centre of the meadow. 'In there,' he said.

'Well, we shall go in there and *un*clap them at once,' said Randalf. 'Then, my dear Joe, we really must get on with our quest for the Goblet of Porridge!'

'I'm afraid you can't,' Deric explained. 'Only barbarians and contestants in the Big Barbarian Bake-Off are allowed inside the Great Hall.'

'Then it's simple,' said Randalf.

'It is?' said Joe.

'Yes,' said Randalf, eyeing the frayed recipe book clutched in Norbert's hands.

A wizard, an ogre and a boy strode up to the black-hinged doors of the Great Hall. The wizard raised his staff and thumped loudly on the weathered timber.

The doors opened.

'Steady on,' came an indignant voice from the shadows.

'We're the Stinkyhogs Snugglemuffin Squad,' the wizard announced. 'We're here for the Big Barbarian Bake-Off.'

'Enter, Stinkyhogs Snugglemuffin Squad,' said the voice. 'And just be careful with that staff of yours.'

The three of them stepped inside.

The door slammed shut.

It was the smell that struck Joe first.
That and the Great Hall's enveloping
warmth. The air was sweet and spicy,
the delicious aroma of baking biscuits
and browning pastries mingling with
the acrid tang of woodsmoke.

High above his head, in the shafts of
dust-flecked light that penetrated the
latticed windows of the onion-domed
towers, Joe could just make out the
silhouetted shapes of birds perching in
the roof-beams. The hall was vast, with
a large round table at its centre and
what looked like a mountain of dirty
dishes behind it.

As Joe followed Randalf and
Norbert across the straw-strewn
floor, he wondered how and where to
begin the search for his sister. Ahead
of them, the small fussy-looking

167

individual who'd opened the black-hinged door raised his large wooden spoon and pointed.

'Excellent, excellent,' said Quentin the cake druid. 'You seem to be the last ones. You'll find everything you need just over there. Oven gloves. Big spoons. Pots and pans. And all the ingredients you could possibly need.'

In front of the biggest stove Joe had ever seen stood five tables, each one piled high with cooking utensils. Stacked on the floor in front of them were sacks of flour, baskets of eggs, and jars, jugs and pitchers brimming with yak-milk, butter, icing sugar, baking powder and candied fruit of every description.

At the first table stood a beefy-looking barbarian in a winged helmet and a crisp white apron with the letter N embroidered on the front. Towering above him at the next table was an enormous purple-scaled dragon, two thin wisps of smoke coiling up from her flared nostrils as she admired her reflection in the back of a ladle. At the third table a peculiar individual in a huge mauve hat stood on spindly legs pouring yak-milk from one measuring jug into another and back again. The heavily bearded barbarian at the next table along stood stiffly to attention, his thick bearskin coat buttoned up to the neck despite the warmth of the hall. Beside him, Eudora Pinkwhistle raised a hand and waved.

'Coo-ee, headmaster! Over here!' she trilled. 'So you're entering the bake-off too. How thrilling! The table next to me is free. Now, what are you going to bake? Do tell.'

'I don't intend to bake anything,' said Randalf with dignity. 'My assistant, Norbert, here is going to impress us all with his snugglemuffins. Aren't you, Norbert?'

'Doesn't that make you *Norbert's* assistant?' piped up Veronica, and flapped from the brim of the wizard's pointy hat on to Joe's shoulder before Randalf could swat her away.

'Randalf, Norbert,' Joe whispered as they took their places at the table and the cake druid turned away. 'Can you keep them distracted while I look for Ella?'

'No problem,' said Randalf, pulling up a stool and settling himself down. 'I'm sure Norbert's snugglemuffins will be extremely distracting. Won't they, Norbert?'

'I'll try my best, sir,' said Norbert, ruefully eyeing the dragon who was blowing smoke rings, and the bog-man who was juggling droplets of milk.

In the middle of the hall, Quentin the cake druid emerged through the hole at the centre of the Round Kitchen Table and sat down upon the throne. He placed a colossal egg-timer in front of him, and waited as barbarian spectators filed into the hall. Pulling up stools and benches in

170

a broad semicircle behind the table, they sat down and looked at the cake druid expectantly.

With a flourish, Quentin turned the egg-timer over. 'Let the Big Barbarian Bake-Off begin!' he announced.

A great cheer rose from the barbarian spectators as the contestants rushed over to the pile of sacks, baskets and jars and scooped up armfuls of ingredients, before returning to their tables. Joe slipped quietly away, skirting round behind the ovens and keeping to the shadows as he began his search of the hall.

All eyes were on the unfolding drama of the bake-off. Delia the dragon cracked a dozen eggs open with a swish of her tail. Pete the Perfumed Bog-Man sent three plumes of yak-milk up into the air like a fountain and caught them again in a measuring jug. Eudora drew gasps of appreciation as, with a click of her fingers, she set a dozen egg-whisks beating. Meanwhile Nigel was making steady progress sifting flour with one hand and measuring out baking powder with the other. Hrothgar, on the other hand, seemed to have shrunk to half his height and was dithering over a mixing bowl, his black beard trailing in the pancake batter he was attempting.

All eyes, that is, except for those belonging to a large black fruit-cake bat that was hanging upside-down from the rafters high above. Its eyes were fixed firmly on Joe as he ducked and dived along the walls of the Great Hall, peering into its nooks and crannies. Behind the mountain of dirty dishes, just to the right of a mouldy-looking lump of cake with a sword stuck in it, Joe came to the top of a flight of stairs. A sign on the wall with an arrow read, *Dungeons this way.*

'The dungeons,' said Joe.

'Yes,' said Veronica, 'the perfect place to clap someone in irons.'

Joe followed the arrow down the stairs. It was dark and dank, with the sound of dripping water echoing up from the gloom. He reached out a hand. The walls felt cold and slimy to the touch. Arriving at the bottom of the stairs, Joe made his way along a low, narrow passageway towards the dim outline of a door. As he approached, he saw that it was thick and nail-studded and, curiously for the door to a dungeon, slightly ajar.

With a trembling hand, Joe pushed at the heavy door. It swung slowly open on creaking hinges. Taking a deep breath, he stepped inside . . .

And found himself in a small, cosy sitting room, with charming floral wallpaper and a thick yak-wool carpet. Two high-backed armchairs upholstered in matching paisley fabric were positioned in front of a small fireplace which was framed with elegant green and white tiles. Ella sat in one chair and Edward sat in the other. Each wore delicate bracelets of blue-grey iron, with fine chains linking them to wafer-thin metal collars at their necks.

'Clapped in irons!' exclaimed Veronica. 'Clapped in jewellery more like!'

'It's just for show,' said Edward languidly from the chair. 'We've given our word we won't escape until we've served our time. The cake druid sentenced me to four days for thumbsucking, and Ella got two days for pancake-battery, didn't you, Ella?'

But Ella wasn't listening. 'Joe!' she cried, jumping up from her chair. 'What are *you* doing here?'

'I could ask you the same thing,' said Joe hotly. 'I've been looking for you all over Muddle Earth! What's been going on? Why did you run off? How do you think we're ever going to get home if you go disappearing like that?'

'Home?' said Ella, a faraway look coming into her eyes. 'You know, Joe, I'd almost forgotten home.' She paused. 'Edward had to disappear, and I couldn't let him go alone. He was in danger. He needed me . . .'

'Needed you?' came a screech from behind them, and everyone turned to see a large fruit-cake bat standing in the doorway, its wings flapping. 'Needed *you*!' it screeched again.

It hunched over and drew its wings over its head. Then, seeming to unfold itself, it rose up to human height and swept back its wings once more, which were now the folds of a black cloak, to reveal a young girl, pale-skinned, black-haired and lovely.

'Edwina!' groaned Edward.

'Ooh!' cried the barbarians. 'Aah!'

'Ooooh!'

'Aaaaaaah!'

With a flick of her tail, Delia the dragon tossed a treacle tart, crimped at the edges and exquisitely latticed with pastry strips, high into the air. She opened her jaws and sent a plume of flame up to meet it. Then, holding out a scaly

175

paw, she caught it in her talons. It was toasted to perfection.

'By the Apron Strings of Lionel the Timid!' a barbarian bellowed.

'By the Measuring Thimble of Stephen the Stumpy!' roared another.

'By the Leaky Buckets of Beverley the Bountiful!'

Peat the Perfumed Bog-Man had conjured up five columns of spinning icing. Each of them danced on the tips of the long stick-like fingers of his left hand while he conducted them with his right. As the barbarian spectators exclaimed in wonderment, the bog-man slowly closed his hand, bringing the twisting spirals of caramel, chocolate, vanilla, raspberry and lemon icing together in a marvellous striped pillar. He clicked the fingers of his right hand. The spinning pillar of icing jumped across to the five-tier gateau that stood before him and decorated it with wavy piping and ornate rosettes.

Nigel Nephew-of-Nigel paused for a moment to admire the spectacle before returning to his chocolate-chip meringues. His once crisp white apron was now spattered with egg-white, icing sugar and chips of chocolate, so that the embroidered N was barely visible. The strain on his face was clear as he pulled on his oven gloves, knelt before the stove and removed a steaming baking tray.

The barbarian held up his meringues in triumph.

'Nigel! Nigel! NIGEL!' roared the crowd.

Eudora breezed past, a line of fairy-cakes flapping after her like little ducklings.

'Up on the silver cake-stand, my light and fluffy

darlings,' she cooed.

At the table next to her, Hrothgar the Hunger Slayer appeared to have fallen asleep. He was slumped forward, the arms of his bearskin coat hanging limply at his sides and his horned helmet resting against his mixing bowl. Not that any of the crowd noticed as the witch, the bog-man, the dragon and the home favourite, Nigel, continued to delight them with their cake-making skills.

Nobody noticed Norbert either as he quietly put the finishing touches to his snugglemuffins. Drenching some with icing sugar and sprinkling others with hundreds and thousands, he hummed softly to himself under his breath. Beside him, perched on the stool and basking in the heat of the oven, Randalf was fast asleep.

On his throne in the middle of the Round Kitchen Table, Quentin tapped the glass of the colossal egg-timer.

'Five minutes to go!' he announced.

'Yes, Edward, it's me,' said Edwina, her lovely eyes flashing. 'Did you really think that you could escape from me? Haven't you learned by now that wherever you go, however hard you try to hide, I shall always find you in the end? Golden Towers, Stinkyhogs, Nowhere . . . I've tracked you down every time, and I always will, because our love can never die!'

'Love?' said Edward. 'It isn't love, it's obsession. You're crazy . . .'

'Crazy!' screeched Edwina. 'Crazy? If I am, it's because of you! Oh, Edward, why can't you accept what you are, what I made you? All those years ago in your uncle's castle . . .'

'Whatever,' said Edward.

'Yes, Whatever!' Edwina cried. 'When I turned you into a vampire, I thought that we would be together forever, roaming Muddle Earth, sucking thumbs for eternity. But

179

no. You had to go and spoil things by running away, denying your true nature, sucking the thumbs of stiltmice and rabbits and little woodland creatures, when you could have feasted upon the delicious digits of royalty with me . . .' Her eyes narrowed. 'It was me. I sucked that battlerabbit's thumb, just to get you into trouble. And I'd do it again. I'd do anything to make your life a misery. I want you to suffer as I have suffered . . .'

'You're mad, Edwina!' said Edward, tearing the delicate shackles from his wrists and neck and flinging them away. 'You tricked me. I've never had any feelings for you, and I never will.' He turned to Ella, who had pulled off her own chains, and took her hands in his. 'Whereas Ella, here . . .'

'Ooh, Edward,' said Ella, gazing into his gorgeous eyes.

'Her!' screeched Edwina, her shoulders hunching. 'You're choosing *her* over me?' She gave a deranged cackle of laughter. 'We'll see about that!'

With a snarl, she threw herself at

Ella, her eyes flashing blood-red and lips parting to reveal two sharp white fangs. But Edward was too quick for her. He sprang forward, putting himself between Ella and the enraged vampire. Edward and Edwina crashed into one another, sending the high-backed armchairs flying. They fell to the floor and wrestled on the thick yak-wool carpet in a flurry of flapping cloaks and

flashing fangs.

'Run, Ella! Run!' Edward cried as he struggled to pin Edwina down.

'You heard him!' cheeped Veronica. 'Let's get out of here!'

Joe grabbed his sister by the arm. He pulled her from the dungeon and dragged her up the stairs. 'Come on, Ella,' he told her urgently. 'We'll get help from your barbarian friends.'

'But Joe,' she protested, as they reached the top of the stairs. 'Edward needs me . . .'

She pulled away and turned, only to be confronted by the black-caped figure of the female vampire looming up at her. No longer lovely, Edwina's deathly white face was contorted and hideous, drool dripping from her bared fangs as she grabbed at Ella with long claw-like fingers.

Ella screamed.

Joe looked round desperately. There in front of him was the golden-handled sword sticking out of the stale cake. Without a second thought, he grabbed it and turned back to see Ella locked in a frenzied struggle with Edwina. The vampire had his sister's wrist in her grasp and was about to sink her fangs into Ella's thumb.

Taking a deep breath, Joe swung the sword . . .

As the broad silver blade sliced through the air, flashing in the flickering torchlight of the Great Hall, Edwina shot out a claw-like left hand and caught Joe by the wrist. With a scream of fury, she dropped Ella and, with her right hand now free, prised the sword from Joe's grip and hurled it contemptuously away.

The sword sailed high up into the air in a twisting arc and was about to tumble back again, when a green-haired fairy in a black tutu and stripy tights swooped down on fluttering wings and caught the sword in a gloved hand. Giggling quietly, the fairy darted back into the shadows at the far end of the hall, where her three companions were waiting.

Not that Joe noticed any of this.

He was too busy trying to escape from Edwina's vice-like grip, which tightened as she raised him up by the wrist until his toes were barely touching the floor.

'Why, Joe,' Edwina said in a soft, cooing voice laced with menace, 'I thought we were friends.' She licked her lips and brought Joe's clenched hand towards her mouth.

'Leave him alone!' Ella cried as she leaped on to the vampire's back and sent all three of them sprawling to the floor.

With a scream of rage, Edwina released her grip on Joe and clawed Ella from her back.

'I'll teach you to mess with Edwina Lovely, barbarian girl!' she hissed. 'And don't think you're going to end up undead like Edward. Oh no, I'm going to suck your thumbs until there isn't a drop of blood left in your entire barbarian body. Then you'll be dead, dead, *dead*!' she screeched.

Her lips opened to reveal her two gleaming white fangs. Snarling, she raised Ella's hands to her mouth.

185

Joe scrambled to his knees, staring in helpless horror.

'No!' he cried and reached out for the only thing to hand—the ancient stale scone.

Breaking off a chunk of the crumbly cake, he threw it at Edwina, hitting her squarely in the face.

'Mffll bllchll,' spluttered Edwina, coughing and choking.

She released her grip on Ella and shot up into the air in a flapping frenzy. As Joe and Ella watched open-mouthed, Edwina writhed and squealed and clutched at her throat. Her face contorted. Her skin wrinkled, her eyes dimmed and her lovely hair lost its sheen and fell from her head, leaving her scalp bald and pitted. Round and round she flew, faster and faster, until . . .

Ploff!

Edwina Lovely exploded in a cloud of grey dust.

Far below, the contestants in the Big Barbarian Bake-Off had been carefully placing their creations on the Round Kitchen Table for judging. Eudora Pinkwhistle had arranged her adorable little fairy-cakes in nests of spun sugar on the tiers of an elegant cake-stand. Nigel Nephew-of-Nigel's chocolate-chip meringues were balanced in a spectacular pyramid on a square oak platter, while Delia Dragonbreath had set her three treacle tarts spinning like plates on the end of three flexible willow rods and was preparing to give their delicate sugar glaze a final toasting. Next to her at the Round Kitchen Table, Peat the Perfumed Bog-Man was putting the finishing touches to his whirlpool and waterfall gateau. It was an astonishing five-tier cake which featured, along with its wavy piping and floral rosettes, a bubbling pool of chocolate which cascaded down its sides and collected in the honeycombed bottom tier.

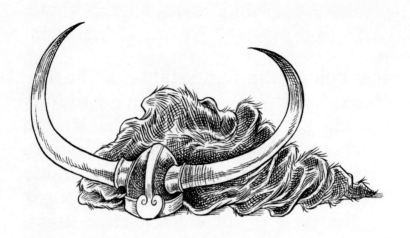

Back at the workbenches, Hrothgar
seemed to have disappeared
completely. His bearskin coat lay
crumpled on the floor, the impressive
horned helmet by its side. Norbert,
meanwhile, was on his knees beneath
the workbench painstakingly picking
up and rearranging the tray of
snugglemuffins that Randalf had
just knocked to the floor in his sleep.
Above the wizard's head Veronica was
flapping and chirping in a desperate
effort to wake him up.

'H . . . Help! J . . . J . . . Joe! In d . . .
d . . . danger!' she squawked in panic.

From high above came the sound of
an explosion.

188

'What on Muddle Earth was that?' said Eudora with a start that sent several of her fairy-cakes fluttering from their nests.

'Sounded like an exploding gas-frog,' said Peat the Perfumed Bog-Man, puzzled, as Edwina Lovely's empty cloak fluttered down and settled over his head. 'Who turned out the lights?' he exclaimed, flailing with his stick-like fingers and accidentally sending a plume of molten chocolate from his gateau shooting up into the air.

It hit the dragon in one of her long-lashed eyes.

In her shock and surprise Delia shot out a jet of flame that set Nigel's pyramid of chocolate-chip meringues on fire. The barbarian let out a cry of alarm and jumped back, sending Eudora's cake-stand toppling off the edge of the table. All of a flutter, the fairy-cakes fled from their nests and careered into the whirlpool and waterfall gateau, knocking it over. A tidal wave of molten chocolate swept across the table, knocking aside Delia's willow rods and launching the spinning treacle tarts into the air. With a *splat! splat! splat!* the tarts hit three barbarian spectators in the front row full in the face, as the chocolate tidal wave broke over the horrified cake druid, who was sitting on his throne, his big wooden spoon in one hand and colossal egg-timer in the other.

'This is an outrage!' Quentin exclaimed. '*Mmmm.*' He licked his lips. 'This chocolate is absolutely divine! But this is still an outrage!'

He stared down at the Round Kitchen Table. Peat the Perfumed Bog-Man's whirlpool and waterfall gateau had collapsed completely and was now a soggy mess in a pool of congealing chocolate. Next to it, Nigel Nephew-of-Nigel's pyramid of chocolate-chip meringues had burned down to a pile of smoking ash, while three wilted willow rods, set in the chocolate, were all that remained of Delia Dragonbreath's treacle-tart display. Marooned in the sticky goo, Eudora

190

Pinkwhistle's bedraggled fairy-cakes lost their enchantment one by one and stopped flapping their cakey wings.

From the rafters high above, the fruit-cake bats and cookie ravens came spiralling down through the air. They landed on the table and fell upon the ruined cakes as the shocked contestants looked on.

'I'm afraid I'm going to have to disqualify the lot of you,' Quentin announced with as much dignity as he could muster as he wiped chocolate sauce from his face.

Behind him, the barbarian spectators groaned with disappointment.

'What, even me?' came a voice.

All eyes turned to the ogre, who was lumbering across to the Round Kitchen Table, a tray clutched proudly in his hands. Following behind was a sleepy-looking wizard with a rolled-up carpet under one arm and a flustered budgie

191

on the brim of his hat.

'In danger? Joe?' Randalf yawned. 'But here he comes now. Joe, Veronica here seems to have got herself in quite a state . . .'

'It's all right, Veronica,' Joe reassured the budgie as he caught up with the wizard. 'The danger's over.' He brushed scone crumbs from his sleeves and struggled to catch his breath. 'I found Ella and Edward!' he announced. 'But then Edwina Lovely found us! She was a *vampire*, Randalf, and she was in love with Edward!'

Ella appeared from out of the shadows at the back of the hall. She was flushed and dishevelled, her barbarian braids falling loose and her tooled-leather breastplate dented and scratched. Leaning on her for support was Edward Gorgeous, looking paler than ever. He was hunched over, his arms folded tightly across his chest, and the cuffs of his billowing white shirt soaked in blood.

'She attacked us in the dungeon,' Joe continued. 'Edward tried his best to hold her back . . .'

'She was too strong for me,' groaned Edward.

'But I threw a lump of stale cake at her and the next thing I knew, she exploded!'

'Exploded, eh? Well, fancy that,' said Randalf distractedly as he looked past Joe at the Round Kitchen Table, where Norbert had just placed his tray of snugglemuffins. 'Always thought there was something not quite right about that girl . . .'

The cake druid inspected the ogre's cakes.

'I have to admit these are really quite eye-catching,' Quentin was saying, prodding the brightly decorated snugglemuffins with his big wooden spoon. He reached forward and picked one up as Norbert watched him intently, his triple eyes blinking with excitement.

'Oooh!' went the barbarian spectators.

Quentin took a bite. 'Delicious,' he pronounced.

'Aaaaah!' went the barbarian spectators.

'Well,' said Quentin, 'it seems we have a winner after all! Errm . . .'

'Norbert the Not-Very-Big,' said Norbert shyly.

'Norbert the Not-Very-Big!' Quentin announced.

'Hooray!' cheered the barbarian spectators, throwing their winged helmets in the air and stamping their feet.

'Who'd have thought it?' said Randalf. 'Good old Norbert . . . Of course, he couldn't have done it without my help.'

'Yeah, yeah, Fatso,' said Veronica, who had regained her composure and was back to her old self. 'Of course he couldn't.'

'Shut up, Veronica.'

'As the winner of the Big Barbarian Bake-Off,' Quentin announced grandly, 'you, Norbert the Not-Very-Big, have earned the right to attempt to pull the fabled sword from the legendary scone . . .'

'Oooooh!' muttered the barbarian spectators, exchanging knowing looks.

'The ancient scone that none other than King Marthur himself baked all those years ago to his very own recipe, the gorgeous Scone of Garlic!'

'Aaaaah!' the barbarian spectators chorused.

'Garlic,' said Joe, and sniffed the crumbs on his sleeve. 'That would explain what happened to Edwina.' Another thought struck him. He turned to Edward and Ella. 'Did he say something about a sword?'

'Come, Norbert,' said Quentin, clapping an arm round the ogre's shoulder and leading him towards the back of the hall. 'The sword in the scone awaits you, for it is written that he who pulls the sword from the scone shall become the new and rightful ruler of the Round Kitchen Table . . .'

'Ooooh!' muttered the barbarian spectators as they followed them.

'*And* do the washing-up.'

'Aah.' They nudged each other and sniggered behind the cake druid's back.

'But what is this?' Quentin thundered, stopping in front of the crumbled remains of the garlic scone, the sword nowhere to be seen. 'This is an outrage!' He spun round, his hands on his hips. 'Who has pulled the sword from the scone?' he demanded.

Joe blushed furiously.

'It wasn't us,' said the barbarian spectators.

'And it certainly wasn't any of us,' said Delia Dragon-breath, looking round at the other contestants. 'Was it?'

They all shook their heads.

'And *we* were clapped in irons,' said Edward weakly, taking Ella's hand. 'We didn't see a thing. Do you want us to go back to the dungeon?'

'No, no,' said Quentin. 'The dungeon's only really there for show. In fact, I'm surprised you stayed in it as long as you did. Anyway, this is far more important,' he said, waving his big wooden spoon in agitation. His gaze fell on Joe. 'What about *you*?'

Joe turned even redder. 'Errm . . .'

'It's not Joe the Barbarian you should be concerned about,' Veronica piped up, hopping from Randalf's hat to Joe's shoulder. She flapped a wing in the direction of the workbenches. 'It's the owner of *those*!'

Everyone stared at the bearskin coat and the horned helmet lying on the floor. Quentin's eyes narrowed.

'Hrothgrar the Hunger Slayer,' he said slowly. 'It seems we've found the culprit.'

'Or rather, we *haven't* found him,' a barbarian spectator commented. 'Because he's not there.'

The other barbarian spectators nodded sagely.

'This is an outrage!' Quentin exclaimed. 'Without the sword in the scone, we can't find a ruler of the Round Kitchen Table, and that means the washing-up will never get done!'

'Perhaps *I* might be of assistance,' said Peat the Perfumed Bog-Man in a soft, burbly kind of voice.

'You?' said Quentin.

'With the washing up,' said Peat, nodding his mauve lily-pad-hatted head towards the great mountain of washing-up in the shadows at the back of the hall. 'Allow me.'

'Yes, yes, allow him!' chorused the barbarians eagerly.

'Well, if you're quite sure you can handle it,' said Quentin uncertainly.

'Oh, I won't have to handle it,' laughed Peat. 'Follow me, everyone.'

Peat led them outside and pulled the doors of the Great Hall shut behind him. Then, with a high-pitched gurgling cry, he threw back his head and raised his long arms in the air. He danced about on the spot in a strange loose-limbed jig, then thrust out his bony fingers and began to sing.

'Burble, gurgle, splish and splosh!
Whirl and flow and scour and
*   wash . . .'*

High up at the top of the valley, the waterfall which cascaded down the mountainside began to tremble. As Peat chanted, his hands cupped and his fingers wiggling, the waterfall began to rise. It reared up from the mountain pool into which its waters normally fell and swayed to and fro in mid-air like a snake being charmed. Then, with a mighty whoosh, the waterfall arched high in the sky and flowed down on to the rooftops of the Great Hall. It gushed over the tiles and in through the windows of the onion-domed towers.

And as the enchanted waterfall continued to flow in an uninterrupted stream into the hall, from inside there came the sound of sloshing and splashing and things clattering about as the whole building slowly filled with water. Peat's long arms spun round and round like the sails of a windmill in a gale as his dance became

increasingly animated and his singing grew louder and louder.

'Pot and platter, spoon and cup!
Easy goes the washing-up!'

Out from the top of the onion-domed towers came a soggy flock of fruit-cake bats and cookie ravens, hooting and cawing indignantly. They circled the Great Hall several times before flying off towards the distant treetops. Behind them, the water gushed from the windows of the towers as the hall filled to the roof.

Peat raised his left hand and clicked his fingers, sending the waterfall back to its mountainside, then raised his right hand. He turned to face the two huge black-hinged doors. Quentin the cake druid, the barbarians, the contestants, Edward, Ella, Joe and Randalf stood open-mouthed, while on the wizard's pointy hat, Veronica stood open-beaked.

Peat clicked the fingers of his right hand.

With a resounding crash, the mighty

doors of the Great Hall flew open and a torrent of water burst out. In a roiling, boiling, bubbling flood, it swept everyone off their feet and out across the alpine meadow. Rolling head over heels, Joe was carried along by the swirling current before coming to rest beside a drenched yak-skin yurt, which had twelve dripping battlecats clinging forlornly to its roof. All around, in shrinking pools and rapidly disappearing puddles, bedraggled barbarians flopped about like beached fish as the water drained away.

Joe climbed to his feet. So did the barbarians. And the contestants. *And* the cake

druid. They all stared in amazement at the cutlery, crockery and cooking utensils that had been washed out from the open doors and now lay in a heap in front of the Great Hall.

The mountain of washing-up was clean and sparkling, and already beginning to dry in the warm sunshine.

Quentin raised his big wooden spoon moistly and tapped Peat the Perfumed Bog-Man on both shoulders before kneeling at his feet.

'Long live King Peat of the Round Kitchen Table!' he proclaimed.

'Long live King Peat! Long live King Peat!' the barbarians cheered, their happy voices echoing round the valley as the flock of fruit-cake bats and cookie ravens began to return overhead.

'Long live King Peat!'

'Edward? Edward!' came Ella's concerned voice. 'Edward, speak to me!'

Joe turned from the washing-up to see his sister kneeling down beside Edward Gorgeous, who was lying motionless on the grass. A damp-looking Randalf sat a little way off, deep in conversation with the rolled-up stair-carpet, Norbert by his side.

'The first time I was pleased, but this is simply going too far,' the carpet was complaining. 'I mean, I'm a carpet. I'm meant to be swept. Occasionally beaten. But not soaked! It's not good for me . . . *Atishoo!*'

Edward Gorgeous sat up. His eyes were bright and his skin had a healthy pink glow to it.

'I feel wonderful!' he said. 'And so, so hungry! I haven't felt like this in years.'

He got to his feet and hugged Ella delightedly.

'You mean . . . you need to suck a thumb?' said Ella uneasily.

'No! That's just it!' Edward exclaimed. 'This is different. This is real hunger. *Normal* hunger!'

'Snugglemuffin, sir?' said Norbert helpfully, opening his large fist to reveal a rather mushy-looking cake.

'Yes, please!' said Edward, seizing it and devouring it greedily. 'Oh, I'd forgotten just how delicious food tastes.' He turned to Ella. 'I . . . I think . . . I think I'm cured!'

'That's what enchanted water can do for you,' said the carpet. *'Atishoo!* But one can have too much of it . . . *Atishoo! Atishoo!'*

'Oh, Edward,' Ella breathed.

'Oh, Ella,' Edward replied and pulled her close.

Joe turned away, embarrassed. Big sisters! One minute they're moping about in their bedrooms painting their nails black, the next they're riding off on battlecats to Nowhere. And then there was this soppy stuff to contend with. It was all such a pain . . .

Joe stopped. He blinked. He could scarcely believe his eyes. There in the distance, looming up on the horizon at the far end of the valley, was a large walled castle. It hadn't been there when they'd arrived, Joe was certain of it, and it looked so solid and forbidding, with its stone walls and high towers, it couldn't have been built overnight.

Could it?

Joe stared. Then something else

caught his eye. It was a small lamp-post that had emerged from the wooded mountainside, its light glowing dimly. It scuttled towards the castle  on stubby mechanical legs. As it approached, the drawbridge lowered. The lamp-post trotted inside.

'Randalf! Randalf!' Joe shouted. 'The lamp-post! I've just seen the lamp-post!'

'Where?' said Randalf.

'There!' said Joe, pointing at the castle.

Randalf nodded. 'Whatever,' he said.

Beneath Harmless Hill, the four flower fairies sat in the flickering candlelight, their gossamer wings fluttering at their backs. In front of them, on a small, moss-covered stone table, next to a tiny battered vessel, lay a golden-handled broad-bladed implement.

'The fools! The fools!' laughed Pesticide, wiping a couple of crumbs from the blade. 'We've grabbed the Goblet of Porridge and swiped the Sword in the Scone right from under their noses. And the best bit is, they have no idea who we really are!' She swept back her green hair and fluttered her gossamer wings. 'Nor what we've actually stolen!'

She reached out and stroked the objects on the stone table with a gloved hand.

'The Plant Pot of Power,' said Nettle, her eyes gleaming.

'And the Trowel of Turbulence,' added Thistle reverently.

'And now for the third of the lost treasures of Harmless Hill,' breathed Briar-Rose. 'The greatest of them all . . .'

'The Acorn of Abundance!' Pesticide declared.

'And where shall we look for it?' they all asked her.

'In the forests of Nowhere?' suggested Nettle.

'Or in the orchards of Trollbridge?' offered Thistle.

'Or the glades of Elfwood?' said Briar-Rose.

'To find it, we must follow the light,' said Pesticide.

'The light?' they chorused. 'The light of what? The sun? The moons? The stars? . . .'

'No,' said Pesticide dramatically, sweeping back her long green hair. 'The lamp-post.'